AUTHOR SIG

With every best Wishes!

Tom Bower.

THAT WAS THEN...
Selected Stories

Also by Tom Barr:

Double Trouble for a South American President

THAT WAS THEN...
Selected Stories
Tom Barr

UNITED WRITERS
Cornwall

UNITED WRITERS PUBLICATIONS LTD
Ailsa, Castle Gate, Penzance, Cornwall.

*All Rights Reserved. No part of this publication
may be reproduced, stored in a retrieval system,
or transmitted, in any form or by any means,
electronic, mechanical, photocopying, recording
or otherwise, without the prior permission of the
Copyright owner.*

British Library Cataloguing in Publication Data:
A catalogue record for this book is
available from the British Library.

ISBN 1 85200 090 2

Copyright © 2000 Tom Barr

Printed in Great Britain by
United Writers Publications Ltd
Cornwall.

To the man on the
Addingham Omnibus.

Contents

1

A Day at the Empire Theatre

Ladysmith, Buller finally decided, could best be relieved by a forced river crossing at Colenso. Redvers Buller felt confident about the outcome, for hadn't he sixteen battalions making a three pronged probe in the attempt to ford the Tugela that morning? More ideally the road and rail bridges could have taken them across at the loop in the river, these had of course, been probed, but withering Boer rifle fire from the cover of the wood on the other bank had forced the Queens and Devons into a hasty retreat. The unplanned rest would allow time for a breather and a re-think. To Buller it was a frustrating setback. He hadn't reckoned on the fire accuracy, mobility and knowledge of terrain displayed by the heavily outnumbered enemy entrenched in the trees opposite. He hastily ordered an attempt by the left prong but it soon became obvious that it was faring no better. In the gratifying lull which followed these early repulses, he decided that only artillery could wrap up the deadly menace entrenched in the safety of the trees.

Colonel Long, an impetuous, some said even a daring officer, totally contemptuous of the menace of any gun which didn't have wheels, hastily assembled, harnessed and then trundled out his twelve artillery pieces onto the open ground facing towards the cross river Boer menace. The fact that he should have held back for infantry cover never even entered his head, or, if it had that day, it was summarily dismissed. The twelve horse teams wheeled the guns smartly into position and the sweating animals were then led off to the safety of a nearby copse.

The layers hastily but methodically prepared the twelve avenging pieces, guns built with pride to level offending forests and any conniving enemy that they might harbour. Colonel Long had just stood back to proudly direct the opening salvo when the Boer marksmen suddenly struck. The gun crews stuck manfully to their tasks, but the position had suddenly become wholly untenable. Caught out there in the open, almost midway between the Boers and the safety of their own lines, they low profiled and fired a ragged, almost random barrage. Soon, however, their ammunition began to run out and the number of men left standing was getting unbearably low. At Buller's screamed command, a bare handful managed to retreat hastily back to the Donga where the horses were tethered. Colonel Long was not one of that favoured few.

It seemed a hopeless situation, twelve valuable field guns, desperately needed to relieve Ladysmith, were sitting out there under the virtual control of uncouth Boer sharpshooters. While Buller, really happier at organising supplies than leading men, raged impotently. Reed, one of the battery captains, gallantly set in motion a desperate gun rescue attempt. With thirteen battery crew and twenty-two trace horses he raced from the shelter of the Donga towards his beloved artillery pieces. Caught between the hope of success and the despair of their impossible position, the heroic little band finally faltered under the hail of withering fire from across the Tugela. Once more they retreated; leaving behind them seven more dead men and thirteen valuable horses. The price of the guns was becoming intolerably high.

Stung to action by this latest fiasco, Buller wheeled desperately towards his hovering aides. There was an immediate response, one of those eagerly volunteering being young Lieutenant Roberts, son of the Field Marshal. As the senior Roberts was rumouredly on his way out to assume overall command, Bullers realised the awkwardness of his position, but the situation was a desperate one, not really the time to be playing favourites.

While the new collection of volunteers hastily assembled spare horse teams, out there in the open, lined up in threatening but futile formation stood the twelve field guns, memorials to the recklessness of the late Colonel Long. Their barrels shining malevolently under the hot African sun.

If courage alone could have saved those guns, then the volunteer force would have soon had them safely back in the British arsenal, but against the concentrated withering fire of the deadly Boer rifles, courage alone was not enough. Two field guns were eventually hitched up and brought back to the lines, but the partial victory proved to be a phyrric one. As Buller stood there watching the dead and injured from his volunteer force being hastily brought in, his mind was an agony of seething emotions. Young Roberts, he was told, was alive, but barely so. Buller groaned inwardly, what would the boy's father have to say about this mess? His hellish visions were interrupted when a wiry young Indian bearer staggered past him with a wounded officer draped limply over his slim shoulders. That was the third rescue the lad had accomplished in these last twenty agonising minutes. He must remember to ask Sergeant Singh, the bearer in charge, that young man's name. But right now the guns were the pressing problem. Priority was demanding a decision about these damned field guns!

While Buller pondered the problem, dusk fell with characteristic suddenness on the veldt. He was invited in the interim to give an interview to one of the war correspondents, a young man he'd seen around the lines, named Churchill. The newsman, he knew, had himself just escaped from Boer detention a few weeks back, managing to rejoin his own lines via the Lourenco Marques route. But right now however, Buller was in no mood for pleasantries.

Before Churchill could even begin to question him he launched into a despairing diatribe.

"It has been a black week for us. First Metheun at Magersfontein, then Cateacre at Stormberg, and now, as you can see, I'm taking a second prize at Colenso. I've had about nine hundred good men killed or seriously wounded and two hundred and fifty or so taken prisoner. To be honest I'm right now considering the idea of sending word to White in Ladysmith to capitulate, and Lieutenant Roberts, you know? the Field Marshal's son, he's one of the men I'm recommending for the Victoria Cross. In his case, it may alas have to be bestowed posthumously."

As the newsman laboriously wrote his dispatch by the light of a hurricane lamp, Buller's thoughts were interrupted by passing footsteps. It was Sergeant Singh, the chief bearer, walking past the tent. On impulse Redvers called him back.

"Oh Singh! one moment please, now that I remember. One of your lads showed exceptional courage and bravery today, young fellow, very thin, slight arm wound. Know him?"

"Yes sir, I know him, Gandhi's his name, reads too many books, but given time he'll make a good soldier sir."

"No doubt, thank you Sergeant!"

As Sergeant Singh departed with a smart salute, Buller collected his thoughts and turned once more to Churchill.

"Yes sir. Some of these colonials make fine soldiers. Now, where were we?"

Next morning, to Buller's further dismay, the tardy dawn unveiled a tragic scene, an empty plain, where last night ten field guns had been. Whereas he himself had vetoed a renewed attempt to retrieve the guns under the cover of darkness, the Boers had not been acting so cautiously. As a result, the field guns had gone, spirited across the Tugela in the small hours by intrepid commandos, men who knew every ford and were the undoubted masters of the inhospitable terrain. While Buller brought together his defeated army and slowly retraced his steps from Colenso, ten of his precious field guns would now be lumbering across the Veldt towards Ladysmith. There they would be used to further pressurise White's beleaguered forces.

In the retreat towards Chievela, Bullers forces halted on the Karoo for a belated meal and a much needed rest. As he left the command wagon to stretch his legs, Buller couldn't help but overhear the raised and angry voice of a distant barrack room lawyer coming from the direction of the mobile field kitchens.

12

Above the ambient din, the voice, a Welsh one, carried very clearly.

"I tell you boyos, there hasn't been a really decent one since Wellington himself."

Buller paled perceptibly through his tanned veneer. It didn't take a genius to work out that the loud mouthed squaddie hadn't been commenting on the quality of the meal he was wolfing down. Redvers hastily washed his face, and, the towel round his neck, clambered back into the command wagon. As he reached for a drink, the whiteness of the towel contrasted starkly with his tanned features.

A sudden flurry of noise and movement out on the veldt interrupted his self pitying reverie. Corporal Oates, the battalion messenger, was being helped from his sweating mount by 'Wellington', one of the support kaffirs. The message Oates handed to him did little to allay his rising anxieties.

The newly instigated concentration camps were evidently having a violent and tragic effect since their comparatively recent launch. Food, it seemed, was scarce, women, children and the elderly were succumbing to hunger and fever at an alarming rate. Again, today, some seventy Boer civilians dead! If the last couple of days were anything to go by, the British Empire and Rhodes's dream of forging a railroad from Cape to Cairo was going to take a lot more time to reach fruition than had been originally planned. Redvers turned to thank Oates for his efforts, but the latter had already left the command wagon and gone outside. Flustered by the pace of recent movements, he contemplated his next move.

Yes! That was it, he would arrange a meeting with Haig and assimilate some of his thoughts. There was nothing like a good traditional method officer to help sum up and sort out this bloody mess. Haig was a fine leader of men, especially cavalry men, and no doubt had a bright future ahead of him in the service of England and the faltering Empire, in any foreseeable future conflagration. French too would soon be arriving, a sound General that, almost as good but not quite as incisive as Haig. In the race to overcome the Orange Free State and the

13

Transvaal, the defending Boer commando's were right now having the upper hand. The protection of their accumulated gold was proving to be a very powerful incentive indeed.

2

Days of Swine and Rosie

It seems only days ago, but in reality it must be nearly a year now since I was being introduced to my first school, St Roch's, Garngad. Then, almost at once, rumours of war had thrown my, and no doubt everyone else's, family into a state of anxiety and confusion. Would Hitler bomb Glasgow? Especially the gasworks, the brickworks, the steelworks or the railway marshalling yards which constituted our industrial surrounding? Would the children be safe in the city? Would there be enough food? Would they not be much better off in wartime, evacuated and among caring relatives in neutral Ireland.

As my father was long dead from MS, whatever that was. My Mother Mollie, who worked full time in the local clinic, had reluctantly embraced the Irish option. Her decision finally arrived at, things had begun to move very swiftly. In no time at all, me, my big Brother John and our Cousin Agnes, all clutching our meagre belongings, were being handed over to the ample care of our Aunt Roisin, just prior to her impending voyage across the Irish Sea.

The journey itself proved to be swift and very exciting. The tram-car ride down to the Broomielaw, the ship herself, the *Princess Victoria*, a looming monster which filled my whole horizon and smelled of cattle; or was it drink? Such excitement for a mere five-year-old, tightly clutching my orange and sixpence. I had then spent the whole voyage goggle eyed, as I watched drunken men urging each other to: "Get it down Paddy, it'll do you good!" And some hours later; the enigma: "Get it up Mick, it'll do you good!" While all around huddled groups and families were in turn comforting the seasick among them; intermittently praying and discussing with dread voices the possibility of German torpedoes.

On land at last, then had come the steam train leg of the journey. Me hiding under Roisin's voluminous black satin skirt to dodge the train fare. Not even the Customs men had spotted me when we at last ground to a halt at the border to be searched. Then, with a squeal and a jerk, we were moving again. First, Monaghan, then at last, our ultimate destination, Castleblayney.

Oh such excitement! It was going on dusk when we arrived, and a noisy carnival and circus were blaring out raucous music in a field beside the station. While horses and donkeys were dragging noisy, animal laden carts in all directions away from the town's main street. We had arrived on market day! The wonder continued as we were ushered unceremoniously into Traynors Taxi and right there and then I experienced my first ever motorcar ride. All too soon we were bumping across the railway crossing, racing out past Hagen's Flaxhole, passing the Blackhill Football Ground, then arriving at the townland of Derryisland and Mulligans' white, thatched cottage. First impressions were of a very full little house, with nearly everyone talking at the same time. Old Rosie Mulligan, black shawled and formidable, was flanked by Katie and Harry, her grown up children. And Roisins three sons, Tom, James and John, a mite older than us, gazed at us with unabashed curiosity and toothy grins. Unable to sustain my enthusiasm, tiredness took hold and I slumped into sleep. Overcome by a surfeit of new experiences and unanalysed impressions.

How swiftly the time has flown since that exciting arrival on Irish soil! Months have seemed weeks and weeks like days. I've even travelled around the county a wee bit. Five months ago James took me away on the crossbar of his old Hercules bicycle to Ballybay for my confirmation. I met the Bishop, got blessed and had a great day out. And only about six weeks ago, I was rushed into the County hospital in Monaghan with swollen

16

glands. Beside me in the ambulance was old Paddy Duffy, a neighbouring farmer. He had been gored by a bull and was bleeding from his eye. I came back home after two weeks but he never did: Well, not alive anyway. And next week, God willing, we're all going into Castleblaney Hall to see the Greatest Magician in all Ireland. A man called 'Bamboozelem'.

I'm getting to like Ireland and now I watch Uncle Harry, his bib overall tied at the knees with twine and his cap askew, begin his day. He expertly backs the stubborn ass between the shafts of the cart and starts to couple up the harness. He grunts a bit when he reaches under for the bellyband. It's Saturday again, and Granny Mulligan is going into Castleblayney for the pigmeal and a few other odds and ends. She never takes anyone with her on these regular weekly jaunts; not even Uncle Harry. Maybe she doesn't want us to know that she spends a good hour or more each Saturday drinking brandy in Hanratty's lounge bar – but we know anyway!

"Away in an' tell oul' Rose the ass and cart are ready, gasoon!"

Uncle Harry always calls Granny Mulligan oul' Rosie. Maybe it's because she's really only his stepmother. I'm all excited as I run in through the half door and round the jamb wall. Granny hasn't heard me coming until I'm almost beside her. She hurriedly pulls the stubby clay pipe out of her mouth and fumbles it inside the black cardigan she always wears; she doesn't want us children to know that she smokes a pipe, we know anyway! To get her own back for being caught she snaps, "What's the matter gasoon, have you seen a leprechaun or heard the banshee or something?"

I choke at the mention of such dread words, but composing myself, finally blurt out, "Uncle Harry told me to tell you that the ass an' cart are ready an' waitin' Granny!"

Rising from her seat behind the jamb wall, she shambles like an old black crow over to the other side of the kitchen, sits down heavily on the long form and starts to rotate the bellows. After two or three clicks from the belt coupling the dozing turf fire springs to new life. Bellows are really great buckos!

"Tell Harry to houl' on a minute! I'm makin' a suppa tay before

I go!"

I rush back out to the yard, crigging a big toe on the way. Uncle Harry is still there, impatiently holding the ass's head. "She's makin' a suppa tay before she goes, Uncle Harry." I'm hopping about on one foot, holding the crigged toe as I tell him.

"Dammit to hell! She shoulda toul' me that before I harnessed the friggin' ass an' cart." He agitatedly shoves his grubby cap to the back of his head.

Uncle Harry then leaves the ass and stomps angrily off in the direction of the hen house. He'll probably be goin' to feed them.

Granny is ready to go at last. Uncle Harry returns and legs her up into the cart. He must have been a bit rough about it, for she exclaims angrily. "Gods curse ye, me legs all twisted!" We contritely throw the pig meal bags in behind her in the cart and it moves out of the yard at last, scattering dogs, ducks and hens in its wake. We listen as it moves slowly on up the lane toward the road to the town, with a slowly receding rattle. When she's at last gone, Uncle Harry goes up to the sty and shoos out the sow that the vet says is diseased.

We guide it down to the low meadow and he sends me back to the barn for the yard brush. It takes three hefty swipes with the brush head before the sow stops squealing. I'm sick inside and hate the vet. The poor pig is just lying there, snout oozing blood, and its sides heaving. When it looks up at Uncle Harry again, he brings the brush down one more time onto its head. It grunts and lies very still, I then go for a spade. We bury the sow; the vet has said not to eat it and Uncle Harry looks very sad.

The excitement over for the moment, I wander off up the field wishing I was as big as my brother John. He's over at Hodge's bog driving the slipe. I wander back to the yard again, and get hen's shit on my foot, not the crigged toe one this time. There's a cow piss puddle beside the dung hill and by wriggling my toes in the amber liquid, I manage to wash the hen shit off. I head for the barn, to check the rat traps for rats. None today, but since the threshing mill was here last week, we've caught nine; and that's not counting the ones that the men and dogs killed at the stacks. At the barns where we store the corn all the rats we caught were

18

big, ugly, fat ones. One had nearly been as fat as oul' Rosie and John said that it looked like her as well. But that's oul' fashioned talk. People don't really look like rats do they?

About five o'clock oul' Rosie returns from Castleblaney. She's a bit unsteady and it takes us about five minutes to get her settled again on her seat behind the jamb wall. We then unload the cart and unharness the ass. It rushes at once down to the ashpit and starts to roll, alarming and chasing the langled goats. Uncle Harry carries in the re-charged accumulator for the wireless and I'm feeling important as I carry in the cream crackers and the red cheese and lay them handy on the dresser for tea time. I'm really looking forward to the coming feast, for praties, eggs and stirabout everyday are all right; but the cheese and crackers are more colourful. Granny gives us all four caramels each from a brown paper bag. She smells a bit, brandy I think, but the sweets taste great.

After tea and rosary, John and me are sent up to bed. We sleep in the loft, under the thatched roof, which is supported by bog oak beams. I'm in bed first, the chaff tick is getting thin again, for I can feel the floorboards with my shoulder. By the light of the hurricane lamp we start a flea killing contest. I'm winning! When John, with a grumpy, "You're a friggin' oul' cheat!" Turns over and goes to sleep.

I lie thinking of Mass tomorrow. On Sundays John and me wear the complete highland rigout Mammy sent us in a brown parcel. As usual, all the town buckos will follow us around. They used to laugh at us at first, but now I think they really admire us – well, just a little bit.

While I'm thinking, it's got dark. There's a lot of noise down below in the kitchen; neighbours have been coming in. A melodeon throws out the first few tentative notes of a long, well remembered repertoire. Sounds like yet another ceilidh starting up. I turn over on my belly, lift the corner of the tick aside and survey the whole kitchen scene through a big crack in the floor of the loft. I relax contentedly, this is better even than being down there.

I know that Tom and James are away dancing at the deck, but

the house is still pretty crowded. There's a six hand reel under way on the stone floor. Uncle Harry is busy opening bottles of stout. Paddy Conlon is the melodeon player and Tessie Mooney, one of the dancers, is lookin' helluva stout in that green dress. A movement behind the jamb wall catches my eye — Danky Lennon, the Blackhill football hero is kissing Annie McGeogh; she doesn't seem to be too unhappy about this. Excited now, I nudge John to tell him about Danky and Annie. But he just gives out a grunt and refuses to waken. My eye ranges the scheme below me once more. Oul' Rosie is ensconced in her usual corner, a brandy bottle at her feet and a mug in her hand. There's a short lull in the music, she's telling Pat Hanratty about the sow. I hear her say above the general crack, " . . . wanted us to pay for the slaughterin' of it and the damn' thing not fit for atein! Would you credit that? I toul' him I'd see him in hell first."

Pat nods a beery approval of her actions and soon they start to bemoan the sad fact that the threshing machine seems to be ousting the trusted flail. Then the melodeon is away like the hammers of hell again, Peter Woods is lifting one of the girls and I can't seem to hear any more.

After that, I must have fallen asleep, for the next thing I know the oul' cock is crowin' fit to burst and the sun's beaming in through the small window situated in the gable end of the loft. It is time we were up for the three mile walk to mass down in St. Mary's.

When we get home at last from Castleblayney, our kilts and good shoes are stored away for yet another week. After a praties and butter dinner, which we wash down with fresh buttermilk; John and me and Mickey the dog rush off to the cross-roads. There the hounds and their proud owners congregate every Sunday afternoon before setting of to rise a hare, or maybe a fox.

When they at last move off, hurling insults at the inadequacies of each others dogs; Mickey manages to keep up with the pack for about a mile or so. He is being prodded on by verbal encouragement from us as we relax at our roadside vantage point. But he's getting on a bit now and after a hectic mile or so, he comes limping back, muddy and tired; but contented looking with it.

As I give him a consolatory pat and ruffle his ear; I'm thinking that when I get older too, I'll have to leave all this behind and return to Glasgow; where there's no grass or baying hounds. The thought has made me feel sad. So I concentrate on watching the pack race hopefully over McMahon's hill field. Mickey, now partially recovered, sniffs around my bare feet with growing interest. Ah, life's just great! I'm glad I'm not in the war. Oul' Rosie says that the war is a holy terror! So it really must be bad. But Uncle Harry, who they say fought a war in a post office somewhere, says that some wars are just and worth the fighting and that 'that frigger called Hitler is a blaggard o'hell', whatever that means. Oh I like my Uncle Harry – he seems to know everything!

My thoughts drift once more back to the vet he's the very same man who told us, when the old black cow couldn't drop her twins, that he could open her up and save the calves; but that she'd probably die anyway during the process. Imagine any God fearing farmer agreeing to such a heathen proposal? She'd died right enough, I can well remember them winching her distended body out of the byre, up the ramp and onto the float. They'd dragged her by the head – but aren't the vets full of funny ideas?

Oh well, school again tomorrow. It's usually a three mile walk each way to Shean School, but there's a plank bridge over the River at Geoeghan's field, which we're not supposed to use, but which cuts the journey in half. When the river's in spate the planks under water right enough. There are goosegog bushes growing wild along Geoeghan's hedge though.

I like school, we're learning a poem called, *Faster than Fairies, Faster than Witches*, and another one about Christ's donkey. But I wish Miss Duffy, our teacher, wouldn't try to make me learn the 'Our Father' in friggin' Gaelic – I'm certain sure that God understands the English version just as well.

3

A Lull

From his precarious vantage point high in the rafters of the old barn, Hans Brecht surveyed the British lines through his war weary binoculars. Not a movement! The bastards were lying low this morning. They were probably celebrating the fact that they'd advanced two miles in the last six days. Hans's sniper rifle had taken its toll of course, but still they had advanced, wave after relentless bloody wave. You couldn't help but admire their guts. They were learning to keep their heads low too now. For not once since dawn had he got in a telling shot. Hans began to day-dream about his home in Dresden – Christ! The bombing rumours just had to be lies.

Crouched uncomfortably in the British front line trenches the infantrymen wolfed rations cadged from a friendly American depot. There was a ration of beer, one bottle between every two men. Routledge, as he sat cynically watching his fellow riflemen, shook his head contemptuously. Beer and American grub. Such was the stuff of heroes. Conned by fat cigar smoking politicians they had rushed to free England's green and pleasant land from Nazi aggressions. The fact that England was being defended on French soil probably never entered their heads. The poor fools couldn't see farther than the next pint, the next woman, or the next football match. And at the end? Home they'd rush to a land fit for heroes. As long as it wasn't London, Coventry, or Clydebank they were rushing home to of course, for rumour had it . . . Here they all were, trapped in a web of fear. Afraid of being

22

labelled cowards, afraid of admitting they'd been conned by the subtle propaganda machine, afraid of revealing their fear to each other. Christ! Half of them reeked of stale piss. The amber badge of courage. Yea! Crane would have enjoyed that one. None of them he'd talked to had really worked out why they were there in that stinking grave of a slit trench. Duty! Loyalty, Patriotism, all the usual crap had been trotted out; it would be echoed in the German lines. Only Jock Morrison, the Scotch bastard in A company had seemed to grasp what he, Routledge, had been trying to tell them. But Morrison had shied off. Funny place Scotland, he'd never been there, but history had portrayed it as a land of genius or cretin, nothing in between. Morrison was a puzzle.

Routledge's thoughts drifted back home the long miles to his neat orderly little study in that cottage deep in the heart of Wiltshire. There, among familiar books, a man could come up with a rationalisation of all the world's ills. The present group aggressions could probably be explained away in an objective atmosphere. Germany's misplaced faith in Hitler probably being balanced out by Britain's traditional tendencies to poke into European affairs and her sense of public insult. And when it was all over? All the misery, destruction, human degradation and cultural erosion, history would repeat itself. What price the laurel wreath of victory? The vanquished of course would have deserved all they'd got, until trade links had been re-forged that was. Then the propaganda machine would smoothly slide into reverse gear. Christ! Why was he here among all this carnage of mud and blood?

One could just up and walk away from it all of course, but that demanded a courage way beyond the call of duty. The contempt of his fellow soldiers? The social implications at home. To be a pariah in a land of conformity, required something extra. And whether that something extra was good or bad only history could judge. Sassoon had nearly made it, Robert Graves too! But did he, Routledge have that something extra? He looked around at his still wolfing mates. Christ! Didn't they realise that for some of them it was going to be their last frigging meal? On sudden

23

impulse Routledge decided that he'd had enough. He'd tried to reach them, now he'd just have to go alone.

He scrambled awkwardly out of the trench, and discarding his rifle pack and greatcoat as he ran, he made back towards the distant reserve trenches.

As he scanned the battlefield from the reserve trenches, Captain Lennox's reaction to Routledge's shambling retreat was reflex and almost instantaneous. With an over the top advance scheduled to take place in fifteen minutes time, desertion was one sore that just mustn't be allowed to spread. Just half a second after Routledge had got Captain Lennox's revolver bullet in his heart, he got Hans's first contribution to that day's war effort in his sagging spine. His legs wavering under the weight of his suddenly unsupportable body, Routledge stumbled and fell. Down, down he tumbled into a black and limitless void. If these people had only read the books! He had been so near and yet . . .

Routledge's inglorious departure had caused a buzz of reaction in the front line trenches. Food temporarily forgotten, the Newport Jones exclaimed to no one in particular.

"Man! Poor old Routledge, owed him twenty fags I did. The geezer wouldn't hurt . . ."

"Aye!" butted in Jock Morrison. "He aye preached Pacifism. But he was making the wrong speech from the wrong soapbox at the wrong time, and in that costume too. Besides, the poor bugger had read all the wrong books."

"What have books got to do with it?" Jones's voice was genuinely puzzled as he angrily threw out the question. Jock Morrison shook his head sadly.

"Well, it's like this laddy! If he'd read Trotsky's philosophy he'd have known that the science of war and killing demands that the front line soldier must be given two alternatives. Probable death if he advances, or certain death should he attempt an unplanned retreat. You can hate the situation, but by God you've got to respect the bloody logic. There's a time and a place for preachin' pacifism. But our friend Routledge didn't die in vain."

"You reckon not, Jock?"

"No, Taffy old son."

24

"How come then?"

"Well, his retreat pinpointed the whereabouts of that Kraut sniper who's been taking our lads out of the game. He's in the roof of that old barn out to our left. I suggest that at the next advance you and I work our way along that ditch there, and have the bastard from the rear. He'll of course get a few of our mates before we can silence him, but as long as he doesn't get us, Taffy boy. To be living, breathing, hoping individuals at the end of each day's carnage, that's the object of the exercise."

Taffy nodded absently in reply. His mind was now suddenly a jumble with nice sounding Bible class phrases such as, loving one's neighbour, and laying down one's life for one's friends. Routledge had been like that, in a way. Taffy impulsively popped his head up to gaze back towards the crumpled form of his late comrade. As he mouthed a silent farewell to Routledge, his recklessly exposed back presented a target which no self respecting German sniper could possibly miss. Hans Brecht didn't.

Just as the lifeless Taffy fell down into the mud at the bottom of the trench, the advance signal sent his mates scrambling out over the top. Jock Morrison, crouched and zig-zagging as he advanced, made for the shelter of the ditch which led up behind Hans's old barn. Jock's blood pounded fiercely in his ears with the dread, and excitement, of the advance. One never knew the minute, the second. But in a way it was good to be back in the comparative safety of the battlefield. Out there you only had one enemy to contend with.

b

4

Time Lag for a Corn Chandler

Barlinnie Prison, known to all and sundry as the Bar-L, stands on the Eastern fringes of Glasgow's steaming metropolis. A bulging grey monument to harassed law and order; it houses more than a thousand men, reluctant guests whose main regret about their stay there is the length of it.

In cell sixteen, north wing, just above the prison bake-house, about to be released Danny 'Nick' McGuinness was having a casual chat with his cell mate Joe Ross. His voice oozing undisguised envy, Joe asked Nick eagerly.

"What time's your interview tomorrow with the new governor?"

"Three-thirty Joe, and I'm looking forward to it like a baker looks forward to hearth-burn."

"Oh, I don't know, the 'vine says he's a gentleman!"

"Yea? Well the 'vine must have developed a wonderful sense of rumour. I'll bet he's as much a gentleman as Ex-Lax is a chocolate."

"I suppose you're right Nick, anyway, I'll be sorry to lose you. Given a wee bit more time you could have got the librarian's job. What did you work at, legitimately I mean, outside, Nick?"

"Well, I had a spell as a weather forecaster up in the Orkneys; but the weather up there didn't seem to agree with me, so I quit. I then got a good position in Edinburgh with this Irish undertaker guy."

"Sounds like a dead end number?"

"Very punny! But it wasn't really. We were on payment by results, and it was a popular time for dying; the boss used to go round whistling 'Mountains of Mourn': But the job was small bier really, and I eventually got fed up sitting on my hearse all day, so I departed the scene."

"You seem to get employment outside, no bother at all. What's the big secret?"

"Well, it's like this Joe. As my friend Runyon used to say, 'He who tooteth not his own horn, the same shall not be tooted.' It doesn't always work though, sometimes you end up as successful as a street walker with fallen arches. I remember once conning my way into a scientific position down in Dumfries, lasting six hours too . . ." Nick paused for a reflective moment. "Then I made a faux pas which stood out like a flat chest in a beauty contest. I really thought that copper nitrate was a policeman's overtime. Still . . . it was a longer track record than my dispensing chemist attempt. I told this guy to pour one teaspoonful into the palm of each hand; he tried it too! They fired me because I wasn't dispensing with accuracy! I ask you, Joe!"

Joe, his voice filled more with admiration than condemnation, could only gasp. "You're a helluva man, Nick!"

"Aye, I suppose you're right Joe. I'm bad, right enough, but not as bad as those who are worse. It's a lack of education really. My old man planned to send me to Agricultural College, but I didn't get my hay levels, hadn't tried all that hard, if you want me to beetrootful. I finished up in a travelling circus that year. Have you ever tried to do your level best standing on your head, Joe? It's hard man. It's really hard."

A rattle at the cell peephole made them look up with a start. But it was only old Whitworth, the screw, doing his regular circuit. Nick rubbed his tired eyes.

"I'm gonna turn in now Joe. I've a busy day ahead of me tomorrow. I'll leave you with the parting thought that sheep farmers never get to know the exact size of their flock – an occupational hazard in sheep counting it would seem."

The following afternoon, as he was being noisily fed from section to section on his journey to the governor's office, Nick was reflecting happily that licensed bars would soon be replacing prison bars. On impulse he turned to Cork, his accompanying screw.

"What's the new governor like then?"

"Well, Nick, he's a McTavish from Peterhead. And no McTavish is ever lavish, they don't cast their bread upon the waters until they're sure the tide's coming in. They say he started off selling ready frayed suits to Irish tattie workers. Then he became a navigator on the tug boats. But he couldn't have known his Madras from his Elba, for he finished up a screw in Peterhead, and he's been in prison service for nigh on twenty years now."

"I just can't wait to meet this long distance bagpipe player!"

Nick was ushered into McTavish's office, just as the latter was attempting to finish off that day's crossword puzzle.

"Ah! There you are Mr McGuinness. You may leave us now, Cork!"

As the screw saluted and made a bolt for the door, McTavish exclaimed, "I'm beat! A nine letter word meaning a highlander's bank. It has really floored me."

"How about Axminster, sir?"

"Axminster? Why, of course, excellent work McGuinness, such a pity you're leaving us. I don't know just where we crossword addicts are going to end up!"

"How about six down and three across, sir?"

"Eh, what! Are you being impertinent, man?"

As Nick shook his head in wide eyed innocence, McTavish picked up a file from his desk.

"Let's see now, Daniel McGuinness, aged thirty, completing with good behaviour two six month consecutive stretches for peddling stolen bicycles in Perth and Saltcoats. A big wheel, eh!" McTavish oozed contempt.

"Oh no, sir! Penny farthings have been replaced by the modern, small wheel variety now."

"Shut up! one previous conviction, took first prize at the Oban Royal Highland Show, for which you got thirty days. A born collector of second prizes! Why do they call you Nick?"

"It's a long story, sir!"

"Your father played guitar, how did you get on with him?"

28

and true to type she'll skip," knew what he was about. Nick studied Charlie's plaintive cry for a long moment. Oh, for the uncomplicated peace of the Bar-L. Only the fact that he was colour blind prevented Nick from seeing red.

As he passed the Hi Hi bar, a beery voice within was encouraging an unseen companion. "Get it down you Jimmy! It'll do you good!"

When Jimmy reached home, his wife would no doubt have some other advice to give. "Bring it up, Jimmy! It'll go you good!" Such was the boozer's happy paradox.

Home at last. The abode next door to his brother's boarding house was occupied by a violinist with a treble cleft chin and a sense of humour. Tacked to his peeling door, for the edification of expected pupils, was a succinct notice. "Bach in a minuet or two."

Once a crook, always a crook. Over dinner, Nick's guarded welcome from his brother just stopped short of asking when he was going back. The elder McGuinness was an ex-boxer. But he had finished his boxing career appropriately named 'Kid Linoleum' by discerning fans. His welcome for his short lost brother had been reminiscent of the mourning after the fight before. Definitely a four letter man.

After dinner, a stroll in Queen's Park perked up Nick's spirits no end. One battling football team even approached him with an offer as a part time, unpaid football manager. Having watched them lose seven nothing, he reckoned that it was a ham curer and not a football manager they needed, so he turned down the offer. For hadn't their only concerted move of the game been towards the oranges at half time. However, they must have noticed his potential to make the offer in the first place. As he moved on, he felt akin to Columbus. Both setting out not knowing where they were going, when they got there they wouldn't know where they were, and when they came home they wouldn't know where they'd been. But who cared! For didn't tailors sew where angels feared to thread! Well, something like that anyway. Maybe in a year or two, given a bad break and a lousy lawyer, he could get that librarian's job in the Bar-L. One had to think positively about these things.

31

5

Murphy

"My brother Vincent and I climbed The Matterhorn, The Jung Frau, Mont Blanc and The Eiger; North Face of course, all in one week!"

Murphy drew breath, burped and carefully studied his audience's reaction. Satisfied at last that the awesome statement had had the desired impact, and that our two faces were registering the expected quota of awe, he rambled on with growing confidence.

"Yes; we were really fit at that time of course – had done all our height training for that little lark up in the Cheviots."

He paused for dramatic effect, fumbled behind his bunk, and the expectant silence was abruptly shattered by a lively hiss as he expertly tore open another can of lager. As he raised the can to his parched lips, his left hand, with long practised skill, was crushing and flipping its empty predecessor into the nearly full gash bucket which lay under his work-desk. No doubt about it, Murphy was becoming a chain drinker. It was only a matter of time before his hangovers would begin to overlap.

Nevertheless we enjoyed the company of the new deck officer and every night at sea, when McGregor and I left the Engine Room after the eight to twelve Watch, we would graduate, via a shower and a change of gear, up to his cabin; there to swap yarns for an hour or so before turning in. Murphy was a great yarn dispenser, and had been around too, if he was to be believed. While his fellow deck officers claimed that in his short life he had

achieved everything anyone else had done, and then some. In moments of humble generosity, he also admitted to the existence of a younger brother, Vincent, who was equally, well, almost equally, talented.

And yet here he was, a man of such undoubted gifts, happy and content to sail as uncertificated Third Mate on the rusting old tramp the *Thurso Queen*; that was certainly a bit of a mystery. Oh well, maybe with all that relentless searching for the next adventure he hadn't found the time to sit for the Board of Trade's Second Mate's Certificate. We never broached the subject of course, it being very delicate like; but I bet his reasons for such an obvious oversight would have added up to very good listening. For Murphy, as you may have gathered by now, could be that type of bloke.

The Third Mate swallowed another gulp from his can and continued the momentarily interrupted conversation with a casual.

"Either of you two ever had a trip on a Polaris Submarine?"

Murphy, reading the negative in our incredulous expressions, raced on with growing confidence.

"Yes, Vincent wangled it for me. He was on the design team for Cruise Missiles at the time. Smuggled me aboard as his assistant during the sea trials on the Clyde."

He paused, sipped noisily, and studied for a long moment the wolf's head design platinum ring he proudly wore on the second finger of his left hand. It had got around that the magnificent ring had been presented to him by the grateful government of Old Russia after he'd single handedly thwarted a presidential assassination attempt up in the Urals. Again, Murphy was to fracture the expectant silence.

"Yes sir, some sub that Polaris! A really memorable experience. Almost as exciting as that crazy time I drove from London to Aberdeen at short notice to join one of McBraynes old cargo tubs. I did it in less than six hours. Man, was I cruising that day!"

As McGregor and I started a mental count of distances and averages, Murphy threw us a slit eyed glance, raking our expressions for some sort of reaction. We must have been showing our mounting scepticism, for he very hurriedly continued.

"I had to borrow Vincent's three litre Jag for that trip of course. The poor machine has never been the same since."

I'll bet it hasn't! By this time McGregor and I were trading speculative glances. For, being engineers, we had some idea about the optimum potential of men and machines. Murphy had mingled the marvellous on many a previous occasion, but in this night's output he seemed to be really excelling himself. It was round about then that we began to have doubts about the veritude of his old veracity as the saying goes. But we automatically carried on yarning for another couple of minutes, pretending in our hearts that nothing had really changed between us.

Murphy, eventually tiring of the mundane level to which the conversation had sunk, agitatedly fidgeted three more cans from the crate behind him; our empties were bang on target, but the gash bucket was now flashing an overload distress signal. At that moment the old tub shied away from an unusually heavy swell, shuddered for a moment as though rolling on logs, turned reluctantly back onto course and settled down. As if on cue, Murphy was off again.

"I don't suppose any of you two ever managed to do any potholing?"

My head shaking negative was closely followed by McGregor's equally emphatic, "Not me!"

"You should try it sometime when you're home on leave. I remember once, nineteen ninety-two if my memory serves me right, yes, late August of that year, Vincent and I entered a chimney over in Ireland . . ."

As he paused meditatively, I, ever the wit, thought of asking if Peat had surfed them out again. I held the flighty thought in check however, bit my tongue, and the Third Mate picked up where he had left off.

"We were all of five days down that lot. On the third day down we came across another exit . . . too narrow to be of any use of course, and we were sitting at the lower end, having a quiet fag, when suddenly we heard church bells pealing, so peaceful. I swear to this day that they were the chimes of York Minster. But before we could verify that; time beat us. Our food now low, we had to retrace our crawls and exit from our original chimney back in the oul' country." Fond memories thus recalled, his voice tailed off wistfully into silence.

McGregor and I were once again bartering pointed glances. At this juncture just to see how far Murphy was really prepared to saunter down fantasy road, I decided to take a hand in the conversation. For I was convinced by now, and I think that McGregor was too, that the bold Murphy was lining himself up for the uncoveted title of Tall Tale Teller of the Twentieth Century. I positioned my tongue firmly in my right cheek, sucked in a deep breath, paused, then remarked casually.

"On this long distance travel subject, have any of you two ever sailed out of Liverpool?"

Neither of them having done so, I rambled on with growing confidence.

"Well it seems that late in the Nineteenth Century there was this eccentric old Liverpool Millionaire guy, seeing that work was short like, he employed a big squad of navvies to start digging a big tunnel under the city streets, just for the hell of it. It was years later before they discovered that one of his workers had burrowed all the way across to Dublin, and was charging the equivalent of five pence for the crawl through to Scouseland. That's why Liverpool has such a large population of Irish extract to this day. The authorities, when they eventually discovered it, had to seal off the tunnel of course. For the ferry owners were complaining about the unfair competition."

Murphy, head down and tongue now visibly straining, took the bait and came, verbally speaking, charging in once more.

"Yes indeed, it's certainly a strange old world, isn't it? I remember in '89 while Vincent and I were touring Tibet in our VW Camper Van."

The Third Mate then went on to enthusiastically describe, in minute graphic detail the two Yeti that had forced them to hurriedly quit a cherished campsite in the early morning mist. After this revelation the conversation was threatening to recede once more to that level of staid reality that precedes thoughts of turning in to one's bunk. But McGregor, albeit unwittingly, veered it onto a new tact when he rounded off a belated discussion about conditions on old time sailing ships with the casual throw away remark.

"It's a good job flogging and keel hauling went out centuries ago. Otherwise you wouldn't find me within a hundred miles of the sea. Thank God for the Seamans' Union is what I say!"

Before he had time to gather up his thoughts and elaborate further, Murphy heatedly interjected.

"Don't you guys realise that such appalling conditions still exist in some parts of the world even to this day! The China Seas are still infested with pirates. And as for me, it's not more than three months since I last got a flogging. OK. You may both scoff! But it was on a Ketch, *The Ranahinter* just off the coast of Indonesia. I had, by a drastic course alteration, just managed to avoid an uncharted reef near Jose Panganiban, when the old man, Goanese he was, struggled up to the bridge. After accusing me of having nodded off or of being pissed, me of all people . . . he always had been a bit jealous of my abilities . . . he got into a rage and offered me a logging or a flogging. I took the flogging; for a logging might have jeopardised my sea career."

As the Third Mate tailed off with an unguarded display of simpering modesty. This latest claim had proved to be all too much for McGregor. The fiery Scot, eyes blazing, snapped.

"Oh stow it Murphy! You really don't expect us to believe all that rubbish do you? You're the biggest ruddy liar I've ever had the misfortune to sail with. Isn't it about time you sorted out your propensities?"

I too was mentally echoing McGregor's accusation when Murphy, his eyes and voice oozing pain and hurt, blurted out the despairing question.

"Don't tell me you disbelieve me?"

His intent gaze, as his withering blue eyes raked our sullen faces, was a study in total betrayal.

"Just what do they feed you engineers on with your daily intake of spam fritters, dollops of concentrated scepticism?"

From that very moment to the day we all at last paid off at Glasgow, Murphy never once spoke to myself or McGregor again. Meeting our every friendly overture with a silent gesture of unrestrained contempt. If you should ever be fortunate enough to sail with him, or even by chance run into his young brother Vincent at any time, please pass on our abject apologies. For in the face of McGregor's heated accusation that night in his cabin, Murphy was driven to do a strange thing. He rose unsteadily to his slippered feet, pulled off his heavy duty white polo necked pullover, and turned his back towards us for our inspection.

For many months after a man's taken a flogging, his back still bears the original angry scars and weals. They run in vicious criss-cross patterns from the nape of his neck down almost to his buttocks. This horrible information McGregor and I gleaned that fateful night from a sadly deflated study of Murphy's exposed back.

Sure, we changed ships, and went our separate ways. But if the Merchant Seaman is famous for anything, it's his wonderful sense of rumour. First, word got around that the Pope had been seen conversing earnestly with Murphy about the latter's recent strange finds on Mount Ararat. Then, a few days later, it was the President of the United States' turn; the great man evidently seeking Murphy's expert advice on whether or not there could possibly be life on the planet Mars.

Some months later, after a rather lengthy silence, rumour had it that he had turned up on television, to be gazed rapturously upon by millions of thrilled couch potatoes; as he nonchalantly described his long harrowing trek across the wastes of Samarkand. This in a positive preliminary search for the Holy Grail.

But, to bring you up to date, the most recent word going round the shipping company has just reached me, adding a welcome modicum of excitement to my rather humdrum existence. I mull the info over as I lovingly tend the engines of the old *Roybank*, out on the steamy Africa-Oriental run.

It would seem that the bold Murphy is about to embark on a new expedition. This, to solve, once and for all, the recurring mystery of the Loch Ness Monster. Thank God Murphy is on the case, who better? With his undoubted talents, that will be at least one lingering mystery that we'll at last have managed to clear up, once and for all! As we face the challenges of the new Millennium.

6

The Dear Dark Days

Added to his multi-lingual gifts, Professor Jones's lectures, which alternated smoothly between two such diverse subjects as Applied Electronics and World Historical Movements, were invariably over subscribed. His enthusiastically delivered intellectual outpourings seeming like the waters of true enlightenment to the keener strata of Binford University's student population. Once or twice the word genius had been whispered with awe in his presence. But as he remarked jocularly to Martin, the old Lab Technician who harnessed up his electronic rigs:

"They're queuing up out there as though lecturers were going out of fashion. I just do not understand it!"

The Professor had learned enough from his long life to be modest, and Martin knew enough about his boss not to even attempt ingratiation by flattery, that way they worked very well in harness. It was during one of his electronic discourses that an idea, prompted by a student's question, came to the Professor.

"If sounds," young Cummings had eagerly asked, "cannot be destroyed, but are trapped in the layers of the outer atmosphere; wouldn't it be just possible to electronically probe, unravel and interpret these sound layers. Thus, we could peel back, year by year, an audio picture of World history and couple it to the Internet?"

"A good question Cummings, well put! The theory is of course not new, being last resurrected about a decade ago by an Italian Professor whose name temporarily escapes me. It was not possible then, but with recent computer and electronic advances, it just might now be a viable line of research for a scientist with plenty of time on his hands."

As other questions followed hard on that posited by young Cummings, it was only after the professor had escaped back to the quiet of his study that he had time to recall and ponder the old chestnut of the sound layer theory. On reflection, the electronic probe and receiver were now a distinct reality. But to correlate culled sound with historical incident would alas be something else again. The real time historical calendar had been put out of sync by Popes, Kings, Revolutions and even farmers. Thus making the true time sequence of known historical events at least a year's work in itself. Still . . . hadn't he time on his side? It was a challenge, to once and for all time, lift the lid? Professor Jones wasn't one to shrink from such tremendous possibilities.

The problems encountered, as Jones's work progressed, were numerous. For a start, only those historical incidents which had emitted sound, recording their very existence as it were, were events capable of recall. This much non audio history would be shrouded, alas, in silence. However, that would be one for the future! The professor had already contacted the electronic firm with which he usually dealt. They had listened, mercifully hadn't laughed and had promised to construct the most sensitive receiver now available, delivery date to be within six months. Six months was fair enough! For what with having to compile the true timescale of audible history, he wouldn't really be needing such a receiver for some considerable time anyway.

The receiver having arrived in the interim, Jones at last completed his true time historical event-scale with much relief, and more than a little satisfaction. The unique sequence chart had taken him almost fourteen months to compile. But would it eventually be worth all that effort? Still, that was scientific research; win or lose, much more honest than following the emotive mumbo jumbo thrown up by history's pseud's. A final perusal of the timescale prompted the addition of red asterisks alongside those historical events which had left a hard, definable audio record of their passing. A worrying problem at this juncture was whether event sound would have diffused all round the perimeter of its sound layer; or whether it would be found lumped in the semi arc directly above its particular area of earthly origin. Only time and some patient research would solve that one. The Professor then carefully sited a rotoscan probe on the roof of his lab, and initiated albeit tentatively, a controlled round of explorative tests.

The primary feedback proved to be no less than startling. By first seeking out minutely recorded and charted atomic explosions dating back to 1944, an understandable pattern was soon to emerge. The sound layer ringing the earth was not itself rotating. And any specially sought out sound was to be found only in the area of the ring above its earthly source at exact time of occurrence. This important fact he had teased out when, during his experiments, he discovered that past Chinese atomic tests could only be picked up by the rotoscan at specific definable times. Moments during which his event charts, the revolving earth, the probing rotoscan and the relevant arc sector came into total harmony. The principle now revealed, the results were encouraging enough to warrant a more adventurous meander along the now audible noise-prints of history.

At this point however, things were to take an unexpected setback. The farther back into history Jones began to probe, the more uneasy old Martin, his technician, became. When pointedly quizzed about his increasingly reluctant attitude, he could only utter, and even then almost inaudibly.

"Seems to me some things would be far better left unknown; maybe we weren't really meant to know all the facts."

Jones gave him a conciliatory pat on the shoulder, but nevertheless sighed inwardly. Poor Martin! His reactionary attitude was obviously the direct product of centuries of superstitious pre-conditioning. History had a lot to answer for, and he was going to make sure that it paid in full. What the world now badly needed was a direct injection of 21st Century enlightenment.

Another more pressing problem was more of a technical nature. Sure, he had managed to isolate and solve the difficulties

41

of true-time, point on noise layer and overall sound identification of the main historical events. But was it really all that clever being now able to probe out the general clamour of the battle of Bannockburn, the guns of Trafalgar, or the trumpets of a Beleaguered Jericho? If an even finer tuner could somehow be devised, would it not then be even possible to unravel, isolate out, and listen in context to the actual conversations of historical figures? It was certainly worth a try. A prolonged technical discussion with his electronics back-up firm elicited the information that wonders were now being accomplished in the receiver design world using a new type of thermal assisted, multi phase diode. Courtesy of the outer space people. It had hitherto undreamt of possibilities; and yes of course, they would manufacture a fine tuner incorporating this new advance and dispatch it to Professor Jones in a few weeks.

When the fine tuner eventually reached them, Martin and the Professor deftly harnessed it into the main receiver and then applied power. First results proved to be no less than world shattering. At Waterloo they listened in to Napoleon pompously declaiming the merits of Wellington's leadership. Then a re-tune brought to them the grim reality of the Somme. Ye Gods! The history books would now almost certainly have to be re-written. That same evening, now alone, Jones unearthed the Battle of Hastings and easily isolated Harold's despairing cry of despair as the dropping arrow pierced his eye, later, turning away from the groans which emulated from the black hole of Calcutta, his tuner came to rest in an ancient Roman circus; but the cries of Lion torn Christians made him reach hurriedly for the 'off' switch.

One hard fact was now very obvious: He, Jones, was master of, and expert on, all audible history. That same evening, the increasingly fractious Martin having stomped out; the Professor decided that the time had now arrived for the official public unveiling of his, till then, secret endeavours. The moment was ripe in which to ponder the moves required to tailor the sick, conservative universe, to a new image and likeness equitable with rapidly advancing scientific knowledge. And, on reflection, might not his

42

7

Antonio Liked Birds

There was definitely something afoot in the town of Cordobaya that morning. Avenida Real was being given a hasty face lift and the lamp standards which had been waiting patiently for five years for the power of illumination were receiving a much needed coating of gilt.

At the spot where Avenida Real and Calle Boliver converged, a stranger, just arrived in town, bought a copy of 'Los Tiempos' at the kiosk and scanned the headlines. So that was it! The President's wife had recently died and the funeral was scheduled for today. He casually turned the paper over, skipping the details and began to carefully study the South American soccer results.

At his palace President Gomez paced the study floor. His restless hands and the indiscriminate cloud of cigar smoke which wafted around his portly person, spoke of extreme agitation. Why had Donna Isabel chosen an unpopular time like this to up and die on him?

Now he would have to appear at the funeral and this uncalled for public appearance was just what some dissident elements in the State were waiting for. Yes! Her timing had been lousy. He moved reluctantly towards the newly delivered funeral suit which lay, casually inviting, across the swivel chair which had long since ceased to swivel.

Por Dios! They weren't going to write him off yet. Not that easily. The people who had elected him deserved his continued existence. The President purposefully changed direction and impatiently shook the call bell which lay on his desk. Ramon, his eager, young private secretary, made an almost immediate appearance.

"Ah, Ramon! There you are. Can you tell me offhand where that double of mine is skulking at the moment?"

"He's not skulking anywhere, Your Excellency. Senhor Garcia, as far as I know, has just been discharged from the nursing home. You remember the Avenida Corales attempt, Your Excellency?"

"Of course, of course. But I was informed that all he suffered on that occasion was a flesh wound. The man's a chronic malingerer. See that he reports to me by eleven this morning at the very latest."

With a deferential nod of assent the young private secretary silently departed. Gomez then stubbed out his cigar, left the study and moved along the corridor to the room where his wife's last earthly remains lay. She looked so happy and peaceful lying there.

"Oh, Isabel, I wish — I wish. If only . . ." But enough of that. He cast a last sad glance at the beautiful face of his dear, dead wife and quietly left the room. His eyes were strangely bright, but President's didn't cry.

Senhor Eduardo Garcia, former Hollywood actor famous for his crowd scenes, was the President's double; an almost flawless one at that. Visage, manner, figure and deportment were perfect. He had no trouble in the intelligence department either. For the much travelled Garcia was even better equipped in this area than the real potato. As for the field of foreign affairs — ah! those North American babes.

His understudy act was so perfect, in fact, that the constantly reshuffling Cabinet members couldn't tell when they were whispering their little secrets to the President and when to the humble Garcia; a situation which had turned the latter into a very able statesman.

Yes, very able indeed. More than once had he been called upon to make quick, on the spot State decisions, when the mistaken identity game had been pushed too far. The one slight flaw in the almost perfect twinnage was an ineradicable mole on the right

46

forearm of Garcia, the stand in.

Now, as he received the royal command in his suburban villa, Senhor Garcia was very, very angry and understandably so.

Six times in his hectic stand in career his bullet proof vest had just saved him from instant elimination. After each attempt, the routine never varied. He would be hurriedly secreted away in that stinking little nursing home up on the sierras. Oh, how he had come to hate that place.

The real President meanwhile making a startlingly swift recovery in a private ward of the lush Cordobaya Recuperation Hospital. He, Garcia, getting the bullets and President Gomez getting the grapes was no longer funny however, and now Gomez wanted him to stand in at Donna Isabel's funeral.

Sure the pay was good. But this, to Garcia, was the ultimate in last straws. As he hurriedly dressed, left the villa and climbed into the waiting car, his jaw was stubbornly set. President or no President, Gomez was going to get a piece of his mind, and then some.

As Garcia was heading for his palace showdown, an itinerant musician, known locally as Antonio, strolled slowly down the Avenida Real, a violin case tucked under his arm. He stopped occasionally to throw crumbs from a paper bag to the few moth eaten birds which continued to inhabit the dried up trees along the hot Avenida.

Antonio liked birds. Now and again he got to wondering how they felt about him, but anyway, he liked them. Now, strolling along in the heat, his tall frame covered by a gaudy poncho and his bronzed face shaded by a large sombrero, he was thinking how he hated people.

An old Senhora in black bumped into his violin case and he stopped and glared after her retreating figure. Some people he hated more than others, of course. Take President Gomez now! Antonio paused again and smiled. Today, he hoped to do just that.

The stubby old rifle in his violin case was getting heavy, an ugly brute of a thing, but the old man in the market place had given him a guarantee that it would do a much better job than the new rifles they were making nowadays. An old man dashed

47

behind a tree further down the Avenida. Was someone following him? Nonsense. Antonio moved on slowly, unhurriedly, for he already had the spot and all the details arranged. Antonio deserved top marks for thoroughness.

The cortège swung slowly out of the palace grounds and along the mule crowded Avenida Real. Next stop the San Lorenzo cemetery. For once Donna Isabel was the centre of attraction.

The horses had just settled into a regal canter when the shots rang out from the Casa Morena Insurance building. In the open saloon behind the hearse the sad, solitary presidential figure slumped into oblivion, his hands tearing for a moment at the blood which seeped uncontrollably through his chain mail vest.

Antonio – for Antonio was the assassin – had graduated at last. But in his brief moment of . . . triumph, he made the fatal mistake of showing himself for a moment on the Casa Morena roof and a bullet, fired by a wildly excited presidential guard, tore its way into his shoulder.

He cursed his brief, uncontrollable moment of exultation; it wasn't really a serious wound, given treatment; but who wanted the treatment being loudly offered by the angry mob which surrounded the insurance building? Not Antonio. Definitely not Antonio!

He had locked the skylight which afforded the only entrance to the roof and now sat with his back against the inner side of the parapet wall. Antonio was feeling weak, but he was smiling happily. An empty Canha bottle lay beside him, and he was pressing the half empty bag of crumbs against his shoulder wound. But still the blood continued to flow. The rifle lay half in and half out of the open violin case.

The sun was just setting when word filtered out from the palace that the President was making a marvellous recovery and was even now slowly recuperating in the Cordobaya Hospital. It would be a long fight, of course, but with his spirit he would make it. In his private ward of the hospital the President nodded his approval when he heard the circulating rumour.

Bueno! He would have to get another double as quickly as possible, of course. A nuisance that. But in politics these things just couldn't be avoided. Only this time there would be no need for a perfect double: that tended to confuse the issue too much. Some one who wasn't too intelligent would do admirably.

The President settled back into the soft bed with a contented sigh and absentmindedly reached out for a grape from the bunch which lay on his bedside table. The arm of his pyjama jacket rode up past the mole on his right forearm with the exertion.

For two whole days Antonio had that roof all to himself. An occasional shot down through the closed skylight panel on the first day kept even the most enthusiastic of his persecutors at bay. There was a strange, hushed sort of silence form the roof all during the second day, yet none dared to make that final assault on his little fortress. But I lie, for the birds didn't neglect their former benefactor. Not them.

First the little ones flew up from the trees on the Avenida for a short while, and then the bigger ones came. Some people even swore afterwards that they had seen Urubu Rey, the great white king of the vultures, stop off to pay Antonio a brief visit. But some people will swear to anything.

They blew the skylight right off on the morning of the third day – with the insurance company's permission, of course. The explosion was so loud that it even woke the dozing President down town in the hospital.

Antonio had liked birds and from the evidence of the well cleaned skeleton which was even now beginning to bleach beside the shredded poncho, we can safely assume that, at the last, the birds had liked Antonio too.

As the excited crowd spilled up on to the flat roof, a dirty brown hand, bony with age, reached out, grabbed the rifle and slipped it under a grimy poncho, items like that were always in great demand in the Cordobaya market place. He would maybe have to up the price of the old rifle a bit next time he sold it though. One had to take the rising cost of living into consideration.

49

c

8

The Predictions
of Ella May Watkins

Ella May Watkins' husband Abner, worked nights with Vermont Electronics. As a precaution against stray prowlers he always left a double barrelled shotgun by the side of the marital bed. To Ella May, it was a poor substitute for Abner though and some nights the minutes seemed to pass like crippled snails.

Not that anything much ever happened in Redstick, Virginia, to disturb the night silence; the clatter of shunting freight cars down by the depot, or an occasional owl hooting in the old oleander, weren't enough to place the town very high in the decibel league. Wednesday nights, after Abner had left for the factory in his old Pierce Arrow, Ella May would have a few of her neighbour women in for a seance. It helped break up the long week for her. And in Prince Vladimir, her spirit contact, they all reckoned she had the greatest emissary of the supernatural ever to set ethereal foot south of the Mason Dixon. All of them except Bunty Hepper, the Mayor's wife, that was. Bunty would have admitted it too, if she hadn't been so darned mule stubborn.

Wednesday morning before Thanksgiving, Ella May strolled down Main Street for the usual after seance coffee talk cookies. Her purchase made, she had just left Harmer's Delicatessen when she almost bumped into Doc Beadle. Redstick's one and only purveyor of health raised his battered old Fedora.

"Mornin' Ella May, hurryin' as usual. How's Abner's rheumatics comin' along?"

"Oh mornin', Doc he's fine now, you sure fixed him up just fine with that horse poultice idea of yours. Any big changes in Redstick this week?"

"Well, we've had three new additions since Monday, I'm afraid we're gonna lose old Emma Lacey though. I'm goin' down that way now, but I don't reckon she'll see Friday."

"That's life, I guess. Does she still live in that nice little clapboard place down by the Depot?"

"Yes, Ella May. Thinkin' of buyin' it?"

"I'm interested, Doc. Well, not me personally, but I've a nephew just got hitched down Atlanta way. He's hankerin' after a place in Redstick."

"I hope you're lucky for him, but real estate's in big demand since the factory got hustlin'. I reckon you'd better move fast, Ella May."

"I sure will, Doc, and thanks for the tip off."

Before the doctor could commence his long 'Shucks it was nothin', ma'am,' routine, she bade him a firm, but friendly, farewell and headed for home. You had to be real firm to get off the end of Doc Beadle's tongue.

When Ella May finally got through to Atlanta on the phone, her sister, Jo Ann, answered with her usual cautious, "Who's callin' please?"

"It's me, Ella May. I just thought I'd call an' tell you there's a house goin' here in Redstick, if young Abe's still interested, that is?"

"He certainly is."

"I reckon it won't be available till next Monday. They could come up then and we'll go look see. OK?"

"Fine. And thanks a million, Ella May, you're an angel. We sure do appreciate what you're doin' for young Abe."

With a quick flustered, "Skip it — he's my nephew, ain't he?" Ella May cradled the phone.

That evening, just after Abner had left for the factory, Ella May's thoughts drifted momentarily down to Newport News. Down there, in the mental institution, was where Uncle Elijah was now ensconced. Poor old Uncle Elijah! He had been the

51

original predictor in the family. He'd been real good too, but something had gone wrong for him. She'd never found out what. It had happened so long ago and all, but she still remembered those little card tricks he used to show her. Her sad reverie was interrupted by a loud knock on the door. She glanced hurriedly at the old grandfather clock standing beside the Dutch dresser. Land sakes! Ten forty already. That must be the first of the girls.

It was the Mayor's wife, early as usual. Bunty, the only real sceptic in Ella May's little circle, was nevertheless always first to arrive for the seance. Even after Ella May had rightly predicted that her husband would be elected Mayor, Bunty continued to scoff at the existence of the spirit guide, Prince Vladimir. Admitted, the election of Mayor Hepper, when it did eventually come about, was a bit hard to understand. Ed Hepper had already been Sheriff for six years by that time, without gaining any obvious footholds on the political ladder. He was efficient, but a bit of a plodder, so much so, in fact, that at the Wednesday seance just before election, Bunty had confided to the ladies:

"This here prediction of Ella May's has just got to be way out, girls, for that guy I'm hitched to is far too darned unassuming. Now, if he could only get a front page leader in the *Clarion* before next Tuesday's election something real heroic – I reckon that just might sway it in his favour. But as he ain't ever made front page on that rag before, I reckon Ella May here'll be kinda shamefaced come next Wednesday night."

Sunday night before election, the Rosenblatt Art Centre on Main Street had been robbed of eighty thousand dollars worth of art treasurers. The Sheriff, acting on a mysterious phone tip off, had uncovered the hidden loot out at the Okiba swamp on the Monday. Come election morning he'd been a front page hero in the *Clarion*. Victory, under the very favourable circumstances, had for him been a mere formality. Everyone had looked with new respect at Ella May, for hadn't she predicted it all? Everyone except Bunty that was. She, having put her husband's sudden good fortune down to mere coincidence, continued to scoff.

None of them had seen Ella May spend a long, frustrating two hours cleaning the Okiba swamp mud from her overshoes after that successful prediction. Just as well too, for they might not have understood.

The other three arrived as she was about to hang Bunty's coat up on the hallstand. As they began to exchange their little items of mundane gossip, Ella May started to set out the seance table. there, just fine! All was now ready.

Ma Brinkers doused the electrics and they settled themselves round the table, their hands clasped in a sweaty closed circuit. Ella May, while she waited for inspiration from Prince Vladimir, mentally pictured the faces of her four companions. Bunty, damn her, would be smiling cynically into the darkness as usual; one of these days she'd show the bitch, and then some. Beside Bunty was old Ma Brinkers, the soul. Since her hubby's death she'd attended the seance regular as clockwork. Ella May suspected she'd just been coming for the company. And finally, there were the Ellermann sisters, Debbie and Cassie. She never quite knew why they always turned up faithfully every Wednesday night. Debbie, a very sensitive girl, had been a promising actress once, but one unkind Hollywood director had told her she didn't even rate the toilet roll in a bathroom scene. The brutal criticism had shattered her and now she worked in Jepson's hardware store at the corner of Main and Fourth. Poor Debbie! Ella May hadn't quite managed to contact the dead boyfriend of Cassie, the other sister yet. She'd been near it once though. Someone had mentioned in her presence that the deceased sweetheart, Arthur, was a miller from down Richmond way. With the Prince's help, Ella May had just succeeded in conjuring up a mental picture of a sad young man in white overalls, when the information was tendered that the 'Miller' part was his name. But anyway, she was still working on it, and as long as the dear girls were happy to come along.

Prince Vladimir was running late tonight. In the darkness Ella May felt the Mayor's wife start to fidget impatiently, her chair creaked. The Redstick medium, searching desperately for inspiration suddenly remembered with a flood of relief her conversation on Main Street with old Doc Beadle that very morning. She tensed herself dramatically and waited for the

53

movement to communicate itself to her hand linked companions. Fine. Then, in her most professional choked whisper, she spoke.

"Welcome, great Prince Vladimir. Have you any message for us from the spirit world?"

There was a tense, expectant silence at the table. Even Bunty, the sceptic, had ceased her impatient shuffling.

"You don't say! When?"

Once more there was an expectant hush.

"You don't say! Thank you and farewell, great spirit one."

As Ella May came slowly back to life, someone whispered, "Ma! Switch on the electrics."

Light flooded the room, making them all blink sheepishly. They then turned expectantly towards Prince Vladimir's sole mortal contact. Ella May, savouring her power for that extra moment, still had her eyes closed.

Bunty, now real impatient for an unbeliever snapped, "OK. You can cut the trance act, Ella May. What gives with this Prince Charmin' guy of yours?"

The medium, smiling triumphantly now at Bunty's ill concealed impatience opened her eyes.

"The Prince has told me that old Emma Lacey is gonna die. He reckons she'll hit boothill before Friday."

There was a concerted gasp of sadness mixed with awe. Old Ma Brinkers, realising suddenly that she herself wasn't too far behind old Emma age-wise, was the first to recover.

"What's she gonna die of?"

Ella May, silently cursing Doc Beadle for failing to mention the old lady's complaint, answered testily.

"He didn't say, Prince Vladimir forgot to tell me."

At this point the tempestuous Bunty could no longer contain herself.

"Aw, nuts! Emma Lacey was right as rain Saturday in Jepson's hardware store." She then looked with challenging eyes at Debbie, the ex-actress. "You should know. You served her, Debbie!"

"Yes, Bunty, she looked real good Saturday."

Ella May glared balefully at the still sceptical Bunty. Well!

54

How could you convince a dumb bitch like that about anything? She should have known better. But she still spent the rest of the evening alternately spilling coffee and trying to talk some sense into the recalcitrant first lady of Redstick.

All day Thursday Ella May kept pushing the memory of that unfortunate seance out of her mind. Late that evening though, after Abner had left for the factory, she got down to thinking seriously about her recent prediction. Poor old Emma Lacey was now probably lying there, cold and stiff, in her little house down by the depot. Such a beautiful garden, but the roof might need retiling. The old lady had probably died all alone too; her eyes filled at the sad thought. But maybe she wasn't dead yet? A mental picture of her very disappointed friends came involuntarily. That just couldn't be. On impulse she reached for the phone book — K L Ah! There it was. Lacey, Emma. She picked up the receiver and dialled hopefully through the new automatic exchange. The dial tone purred in her ear — seven times it purred, but no answer. Ella May was just about to recradle the receiver in triumph when, to her great disappointment, there was a familiar click and a weak old voice answering at the other end.

"Emma Lacey here. Who's callin' please?"

Ella May, choking back her anger, managed to reply with saccharin sweetness.

"It's me, Mrs Lacey, one of your neighbours, Ella May Watkins. Doc Beadle was tellin' me you haven't been too fine, so I thought I'd just call to see how you've been keepin' an' all."

"Oh, that's real neighbourly of you, Mrs Watkins. Doc was tellin' me only an hour ago that I've made a real Jim Dandy recovery since he examined me Wednesday. Now ain't that somethin'? He reckons there's a good few years left . . ."

But Ella May heard no more. She let the old woman cackle happily into her ear for the next few minutes, all the time seeing young Abe's disappointed face mirrored in her thoughts. Abe, whom she had never let down before. And then there was Bunty – she would have to face her too, the mental picture conjured up of a gloating, triumphant Bunty made her shudder. Old Emma got tired of talking eventually and Ella May bade her an abrupt

55

goodnight, the phone clattering gratefully into its cradle from her agitated hands.

For the next five minutes she wandered round the house, cursing first Doc Beadle and then Bunty. After she had regained her cool, however, her face took on a calm, thoughtful expression. She absentmindedly made the fire safe. A glance at the grandfather clock told her it was eleven ten. The rain was drumming on the roof. Ella May reached for her coat, her hat and then her overshoes – yes, she had her keys.

She picked up the shotgun by the bed, went out, locked the door behind her and moved purposefully into the dark, wet night. From the rail depot there came the impatient toot of a shunting locomotive. But she had nearly fifty minutes left. Plenty of time to make good that darned prediction.

9

Don't Kick the Embers

The lonely, anxious looking and decidedly furtive little figure hobbled in and folded, cross-legged, mid the sand and camel dung, in the Souk at Al Arish. A small brown nut of a man, his wizened face was framed by a flowing white beard. His only clothing was an off-white, roman style toga, and onto his dusty feet clung the frayed remnants of what once had been rope sandals. His staring eyes, blue in colour, studiously ignored the milling camel drivers, their ungainly animals and the general market throng; as he gazed fiercely towards far distant horizons. The colourful crowd, in their turn, took one cautious look at his huddled figure and sidled purposefully past. For might not a sleight of hand begging bowl suddenly materialise from somewhere within his shapeless garment? All men it would seem harbour certain samenesses the world over.

In the intense noon heat, frantic sand flies ran amok, and the dung of a thousand camels incensed the cloying, sweaty atmosphere. The little man, slowly raising his head in the direction of the harsh relentless heavens, suddenly cried out:

"I halted once, but for a moment, the sands of time, and gazed triumphantly upon eternity. Which one among you dares claim equality?"

Amazed at the power his voice commanded, the passing crowd stream began to clot. The gathering marketeers now gradually fell silent, some with quizzical smiles on their handsome, bronzed faces; the countenances of others emanating a sort of child-like

57

curiosity, bordering on wonderment. For a long few moments his lancing gaze scanned the innermost depths, ay, even the souls of his now captive audience. It were as though a veil had been drawn back from the very beginnings of life itself. An air of expectancy seemed to take hold and surge through the ranks of the rapidly expanding throng. The old man, seemingly unconscious of his flare for the dramatic, raised his head once more and spoke out strongly:

"I have trod the wastes of Samarkand, and the whole hot sea of the great Sahara has cringed beneath my weary feet. Who, amongst you now, has dared attempt the same?"

He paused, his old head cocked sideways in an attitude which could best be described as challenging. But none of his listeners claimed equality. Satisfied, he continued:

"Twice have I sailed the seven seas, and many more; and I have viewed with awe the works of men of every hue, who here can say the same?"

Still none answered, his voice now flagging somewhat, he continued with some effort:

"Blessed is the woman who has forgotten the recipe for tongue and cold shoulder, for hers will be a happy abode. And as for the men; blessed is the man who goes through life expecting nothing, for he indeed shall not be disappointed. For the manipulations of more than Allah are setting the stamp on men's destiny. For economic Empires never sleep."

As the milling mass began to smile, he continued:

"I have seen desire well up in every heart, for mankind is rational in all things except his passions. But only on the faces of the dead have I perceived fulfilment. Though hot are the blown winds of passion; alas, they too now cool before my saddened eyes. Who there among you would jeer me liar?"

The silent crowd, uneasy now under the mad-like intensity of his sweeping gaze, began to take a shuffling step backwards. Still none dared to voice dissent.

"Yes, I have lived too long, and my constant plea to Allah is a simple one . . . 'Please don't kick the embers' . . . But still he would spur me on. For I ask you, is there even one among you who is really Master of himself or of his own destiny?"

He obviously expected no answer, for he lowered his gaze and sat in quiet stillness for what seemed to be an eternal moment. His shoulders, now rounded and bent, looked as though the sorrows of all Africa and the entire world were resting upon them. Then, abruptly, his voice now betraying a new hope, a new gentleness, he continued with some effort:

"I have lived the four ages of man, and I have no desire; nor does my broken body, to repeat them. There was the age of my childhood, when all the world was a play-hour from the sun's rise to its setting and penitent parents warded off the thorns of grim reality. For both their penitence and their protection I thank them. They are now, I am sure, in the bosom of Allah. I then came to the age, the dream, of personal desire. An age of ambition, where want swallows up need, a time worse even than the cancer that is consuming the vitals of yonder unfortunate camel."

He pointed with bony finger towards an obviously sick camel which had become entrapped by the now milling throng.

"When that age of greed, not need, eventually passed away, I began to live again. Then came that glorious balm which indicates the arrival of the third age. An age of internal peace and resignation. At first I accepted it reluctantly. But now, in retrospect, I wish I could have lived forever in that part of my existence. Alas, it was not to be, Allah had spoken! You now find me here amongst you in my final age – my age of wisdom. Don't mock me! for I paid for my wisdom with a broken body and a tear riven heart. Wisdom, the final gift. Many charlatans, imbibers of mere knowledge, lay claim to this gift. They, my friends, be fools! For wisdom is as abundant as are humpless camels in the world of both the ignorant and the young. The young we can forgive, they are impetuous. The ignorant we cannot, them we may only excuse. Would any here among you deny this?"

Without pausing this time to accommodate any answer to his challenging question, he drew a deep breath through flared nostrils and spoke again, his tired voice now almost reduced to a confidential whisper. The crowd craned forward, hanging now on his every word:

59

"All men are afraid now. This one afraid of life, that one afraid of death. For a while, sometimes with drink, drugs, they can bury that fear which lurks within their hearts. As there can be no day without a vanquished night, so none can be called brave who have not challenged fear. History, if written by the winners, stretches credibility. Not all lost wars are defeats. Some among you will say I compromise. These are not the wise ones in your midst."

His attempts at further discourse were abruptly interrupted by an angry shout from the periphery of the milling throng. Two khaki clad, armed policemen, swinging batons, began to elbow their way through to where he was sitting. When they finally reached him, the impassive old story-teller remained calm and composed in the face of this angry intrusion. The older of the two lawmen, unable or unwilling to control the anger in his voice, said mockingly:

"So this is where you finished up, you old goat!"

He then turned towards the restive crowd:

"I suppose old Yussuf's been enthralling you with his weird and wonderful intellect? He's famous for his prophecies! Did he not also mention that he slipped out of the mental hospital last night? Did you forget to tell them that Yussuf? Tut, Tut, suffering pangs of selective memory again; some people call that lying you know!"

The old man, his eyes now closed resignedly, remained impassively silent.

"Why is such a wise old man locked up?"

The question was put by a swarthy camel driver who was kneeling on one knee at the forefront of the crowd.

"Because he tried to murder his youngest wife: a fine, educated girl from Khartoum."

The policeman gazed down upon the small, huddled figure and said mockingly:

"Isn't that true Oh Great Wise One?"

The old man, opening his eyes, gazed fearlessly up at the towering policeman. Then, suddenly smiling through broken yellow teeth, he replied:

"It is of course true Effendi; but I only tried to murder her

60

once, and I was drunk at the time!"

As the crowd began to laugh uneasily, he continued:

"And anyway my friend, he who would filter truth through eyes devoid of wisdom can hope only to dispense the law; justice being something else. For even truth itself is not all. In my defence I say that a man's wife can prove sometimes to be only as faithful as his purse is deep. And as for her fecundity, protected if she wishes by a pillbox or a latex castle, no fruit can possibly ensue. She was a young woman whose torrents of spring proved to be gall. They say she works in Cairo now."

As he stopped talking, the older policeman savagely jerked Yussuf to his feet. This accomplished, he and his companion then half dragged, half carried the unresisting old man through the reluctantly parting throng, and headed purposefully towards the nearby police compound. The show, for them at least, was now over.

As the throng began, somewhat shamefacedly to disperse, one spectator began to cackle with uneasy hilarity:

"I knew all along he was a fool, for what wisdom could come from a broken old failure like that?"

"Maybe it's you who are the fool, garrulous one; for he who has never yet failed, has never yet succeeded. The continuum of life requires that everything have two ends. Only in total incarceration can one find total freedom."

With this strange rejoinder, the till now kneeling camel driver rose angrily to his feet, aware somehow that physical war was the last link in the chain of political diplomacy.

The departing crowd, amazed at this final astounding outburst, gazed quizzically in his direction for a long moment, but the camel driver was disinclined to further utterance. So they drifted into small groups and slowly wandered away.

The same camel driver, now alone, stood for a long while gazing at the depression in the sand where the old man had so recently sat. Then he too turned slowly and walked away. His sick camel, with its ungainly stride and putrid breath, following along protestingly in his wake.

From the heights of his peeling, stork infested minaret, a

Meuzzin with a cracked voice began to urge his flock to routine prayer. His tired tones betraying a belief much short of faith. A few moments later there was a scuffle amongst the market crowd, then three noisy young boys, all attired in colourful Djellabas, burst excitedly clear of the milling throng. In their 'Will Be' age of development, they were pursuing a game which looked suspiciously like tag. For a brief moment they converged in a laughing, tumbling, shrill voiced heap. When they eventually moved on, the impression left by the old man's bones had been obliterated forever from the sand by their quick, excited young feet.

10

A Process of Elimination

With a vigorous shake and a cup of scalding tea, Attwood's landlady eventually brought him back to life. He groaned in agony. Oh, hell! it must be Monday again. Saturday was a vague memory of Benny's lounge bar. And Sunday? Sunday was at this moment in time a hangover shrouded blur. Those damned hangovers were beginning to overlap. One hand on his throbbing head, he pivoted gingerly out over the side of the bed. As he staggered towards the washbasin, his legs started to draw circles on the bathroom floor. Boy, oh boy, never again. He peered at himself for a long moment in the mirror. Ye horrors! His eyes were like road maps; he closed them hurriedly and drew a shaking hand down his ashen face. Should he shave? His hand began to shake more violently at the reckless thought. It would wait. Attwood washed hastily and began the long climb into his clothes.

Out in Oxford Street he sprinted and managed to board a cruising cab, but the sudden exercise nearly floored him. He had to lie back, wheezing in the fuggy interior for a minute or two before he could gather the strength to light a cigar. There, that was better, the first one of the day was always the best. He exhaled expansively and gave the driver a Soho address.

Fifty yards from the office block which they used as a cover he parted company with the cab. With an effort he completed the journey and took the lift to the fifth floor. Farther down the corridor he turned the handle of a door marked 'Frozen Imports

Ltd'. That was a real belly laugh! But you couldn't really paint 'Spymaster and Political Assassin' on an office door these days, could you, now? In this little game one had to be devious just to stay alive. And Attwood, at the ripe old age of forty-two, was now head of Department K – a visible tribute to his unsurpassed deviousness.

As he entered the office, Miss Briggs answered his forced "Hi, there!" with a frosty "Good morning!" and a pointed glance at the clock. Old bitch! She very obviously disapproved of his night life. It was rumoured though that she had the ear of the commissioner, so he'd better be careful. Or should it be devious? He laughed out loud at his private little joke, burped noisily, made a rude gesture towards her industriously bent back, and started to open the mail on his cluttered desk.

The first letter opened contained a demand note from double agent Stetsko Grigoryvich in Moscow. It had a Swedish stamp and postmark. Attwood studied the letter for a moment, Stetsko was really becoming too expensive to employ. As for his information, the last piece had been useless. Who in this game wanted to know the amount of salt shipped from Siberia each year anyway? Yet, it looked as if friend Stetsko was due a nice little betrayal. But how? Ah yes, that was it! Attwood would send him on two or three good solid capitalist tomes through the regular post and get him to explain them away to the Soviet secret police. One could always leave the choice of books to Miss Briggs; the arrangement of betrayals was her speciality. "Yes, indeed, we've come a long way since the kiss on the cheek routine," Attwood reflected cynically, as he laid the agent's demand note to one side.

Most of the other mail was routine inter-departmental bumph. But when he opened the last letter on the desk it almost floored him; it bore the Commissioner's personal seal, and read, starkly:
'DESTROY PICKERSGILL, HE'S NOW A DEFINITE
THREAT TO NATIONAL SECURITY. STOP.'
Well, well, Pickersgill of all people. He was seconded to Department Z and was recognised in the service as the only man who came anywhere near to matching Attwood's own success in

64

the espionage business. Attwood brushed aside a pang of sorrow – with Pickersgill's departure from the scene the challenge to his kingship would be eliminated. And just what was wrong with that? To the obvious annoyance of Miss Briggs, he swung his legs up on to the desk and crossed them. He then closed his eyes, thrust his hands deep into his trouser pockets, and began to sort out his plans with a deceptive casualness.

Who would be best for the assassination job? Well, there was good old Pederson, but he was out on the Middle East beat at the moment. So that let him out. Doyle was, of course, busy checking out the Soviet fleet up in Murmansk. And Hope was ferreting out info in the Hangchow area. So that left Greeb or himself to eliminate Pickersgill. Greeb he mentally dismissed almost immediately. He would be useful in the preliminaries, but as for the coup de grâce, negative. Greeb was all brawn and no brain. This job, to appear accidental, required a man with the deviousness of someone like himself. A smile flitted across his shut eyed face. It would be himself, and it would be a pleasure. The decision made, his head nodded; Miss Briggs' tut-tut of annoyance going unheard.

For the rest of that week he had Greeb making careful, unhurried reports about Pickersgill and his regular habits. The file, with his proposed victim's picture gummed to the cover, gradually grew. Pickersgill dined daily at the 'Bamboo' restaurant in Edgware Road. A constant situation to plan the little 'accident' on, was the fact that his target left the restaurant every day about two, and would then stroll back to his office. Pickersgill was carelessly regular in his habits.

Attwood closed the file on the Friday; as he studied Pickersgill's intelligent face peering out of the picture, he decided that he would do the job on the coming Tuesday. The Monday didn't really give him ample time to recover from the habitual weekend spree which he had in mind. And anyway, a day longer wouldn't make all that much difference. The decision finalised, he felt easier in his mind. It was Friday, it was noon, it was time for his usual pick-me-up at Benny's place. Spies were expected to operate on a seven day week basis, but for men with the deviousness of Attwood, five days of concentrated effort in any one week were more than sufficient. It was a routine assignment now. Pickersgill would be hit on Tuesday as planned.

His weekend was, if anything, even more vague than any previous one had been. The only memory of it was a blurred picture of a beautiful brunette called Maggie. Again, it had been Benny's place, and he recalled that she had asked him what he did for a living. He hoped fervently that he hadn't told her. There had been another girl, too. What had she called herself again? Sylvie? Oh hell, who cared! He wondered if he'd seen any of them home, but it was all a blank, and he gave up the hopeless struggle with his protesting memory.

Attwood spent the Monday morning trying to shake off the usual weekend hangover. The mail cleared up, the morrow's Pickersgill affair began to tumble round in his tired brain.

At noon he gave up the struggle; despite Miss Briggs' protest that an urgent dispatch had just arrived from the Far East, he grabbed his hat and headed down town to Benny's bar and that, oh so needed, bracer. Business could surely wait for an hour or so.

Fat, amiable Benny of the constant smile affliction refilled Attwood's glass and continued where he'd left off.

". . . came in, grave-digger up at the cemetery he was, ordered a half pint and then started to complain about not having buried a living soul for weeks. I ask you?"

Attwood smiled mechanically. His mind was busy working on where he could get a vehicle for tomorrow's little accident. A taxi would be ideal, and wouldn't be too conspicuous in a hurried getaway. He glanced up at the clock above the bar – a quarter past one. Damn! He was going to be late again. But not if he could grab a taxi, at governmental expense of course, for the trip back to the office. His glass now empty, and his mind a-buzz with assassination problems, he bade Benny a casual farewell and left the bar.

As he reached the pavement there was a cab just pulling out about twenty yards up the road. A bit of good luck at last. On the journey uptown he'd sound out the driver about borrowing his taxi tomorrow for a couple of hours. If he flashed enough money, the difficulties were sure to melt away. They always did. Attwood hailed the cab. And, as it came towards him, he stepped to the pavement edge to await its arrival – that was funny, it wasn't stopping! He had a final momentary recollection of the cab driver's face as the vehicle accelerated suddenly, mounted the pavement, hit him, and tossed his broken body against a lamp standard. As the heavy cab regained the roadway. Attwood crumpled into a blood-soaked heap of nothing. The vehicle then swung, with a beautifully controlled skid, up the first side street on the left and sped off. It had been as simple and as swift as that. No vehicle number had been taken, and, as the crowd began to gather round Attwood's still figure, no one seemed to have really witnessed the accident. Angry speculation was just starting to take control when a furtive little man joined the group on the now clotted pavement and asked aggressively:

"Is he dead?"

The crowd nodded a shocked affirmative.

"Well, it was his own ruddy fault. I saw him step out in front of the cab! The driver didn't stand a chance."

They murmured a concerted agreement. The driver should have stopped, of course – he had obviously panicked. But dead jay walkers were just gamblers who'd reached the end of a winning streak. Instead of getting across, they eventually got a cross.

It was Tuesday, the day following Attwood's untimely demise.

"The Commissioner wants to have a word with you!"

Pickersgill had just returned from lunch at two when he got the urgent message. He at once made his way up to the old man's office. As the secretary ushered him in, the Commissioner raised his snowy head from the newspaper on his desk.

"Ah, there you are, Pickersgill. Come in, young man. Grab a seat. I see you made the front page yesterday!" As he spoke he preferred the newspaper to his youthful companion, pointing out with the stem of his pipe the six line report of Attwood's death as he did so.

"A very nicely contrived and executed job, if I may say so. Our Mr Attwood was starting to give us some concern with his – er –

casual approach. Brilliant in the art of deception, of course. None better. But a little bit too slow, too erratic. We're flexible in our methods, but there are limits – yes, indeed, there are limits. Our only concern now is the police. It'll be deuced awkward if they suspect anything."

"I hardly think they will, sir," Pickersgill's voice was sugar smug. "One of my men was at the scene of the – er – 'accident'. He's sure to have convinced any eye witnesses that it was Attwood's own fault. He's an expert at that. But I'm a bit puzzled, sir. Just before I hit him, he seemed to recognise me. Do you think he could have guessed that we were after him?"

The Commissioner cleared his throat.

"Well, possibly. For on the day you got the message to – as it were – prove yourself, Attwood received one, too. One which gave him the chance to redeem himself. He'd been slowing up a wee bit recently; getting careless, this we knew, of course; for we, too, have our sources, you know. Yes, indeed, we took a calculated risk. Attwood, alas, is now beyond redemption.

"And you, young man," the Commissioner, his face beaming, threw Pickersgill an encouraging smile, "You have, in the order of things, proved yourself. With this in mind, we've decided to offer you control of Department K. Miss Briggs, your assistant there, will show you the ropes at first. You'll find her a very able woman." The Commissioner closed his eyes reflectively for a long moment. "Yes, indeed, a very able woman."

As he now looked enquiringly across at Pickersgill, the latter's beaming smile, a mixture of happiness and triumph, was the only answer the Commissioner required.

Pickersgill arrived at the office marked 'Frozen Imports Ltd' at exactly nine o'clock the following morning. Miss Briggs greeted him with a not too unfriendly "Good morning," and, when he wasn't looking, studied his reflection in the carefully polished chrome penholder at the side of her desk. Being the efficient secretary that she was, she had already destroyed the late Attwood's carefully compiled file on her new boss. Young Mr Pickersgill might not have appreciated the humour. Greeb, too, had also been pointedly forewarned. Now, as she peered at the industrious reflection of Pickersgill in the penholder, she came to the decision that, though young for the job, he would do for the time being. But if he ever got round to making even one rude gesture behind her back . . .

11

. . . Nor Any Drop to Drink

As he clung tenaciously to the bridge rail of the *Celtic Trader*, Norman Jones, the third mate, silently cursed the darkness; this, as the force ten gale rattled alarmingly the old ore carriers superstructure . . .

In retrospect, from the moment they'd slipped moorings in Glasgow at the start of the round voyage, the ship seemed to have been beset by ill luck. The crew, a bunch of very voluble residents of that no mean city, had enlisted at the merchant marine offices for a quick fourteen day round trip to Murmansk. On arriving noisily aboard, and expecting to eventually meet conditions of nearly 40° below, with attendant pack ice and frozen oil lines; they had come suitably prepared. Packed deep within their bulky gear was the odd secreted bottle of cheap hooch. Crew members were banned from imbibing alcoholic beverages while at sea; but hey ho, who was going to know?

As they'd slipped not quite majestically down the Clyde on the evening tide, they'd cut back to 'half ahead' to reduce wash as they'd passed the looming bulk of Dumbarton Rock. A few minutes later, the ship's tannoy had crackled out its cynical message.

"Now hear this, this is your Captain speaking; change of orders, change of orders! This vessel has been re-scheduled. *Celtic Trader* is now bound for Mauretania! Repeat, Mauretania! End of message." No hint of apology, no explanation from the usually friendly Captain McLean. Such were the modern methods used by unscrupulous ship owners to press gang unwary seamen. Apart from the fact that Mauretania was a country on the West African Coast, which entailed a nine day longer round trip; the gear they had shipped aboard was going to go down a real treat on that hot, foetid shoreline. The crew had grumbled of course, who wouldn't? But the shipping company's ploy had had legal status. And anyway, the tannoy had only afforded one way communication.

On the third day out from Glasgow's ore quay, a calm sunlit day, Frank Kelly, the fourth engineer, on the twelve to four watch, had been approached by his donkeyman in a conspiratorial manner. The crew were planning an off watch Birthday Party; for one of the deck hands like, but non-officer crew were banned from having alcoholic liquor while they were at sea – so terribly unfair! Did Frank think he could possibly aid them in their moment of abject need?

Frank Kelly, a product of the historically infamous Red Clyde, could; and he did! Twelve hours later the said donkeyman became the proud but surreptitious possessor of two bottles of Old Grouse with which to lubricate the looming off watch festivities down aft in the crews' accommodation. All this courtesy of Frank's socialist tendencies and his otherwise unused mess bill.

Such generosities can alas sometimes spawn negative repercussions however, and the fourth engineer didn't have long to wait for these. Twenty-four hours after getting the golden nectar, the said donkeyman had failed to arrive for his watch below. Frank, deciding to cover up the unfortunate lapse, said nothing. Instead he had quietly attempted to perform the duties assigned to both of them. In one brief moment of inattention however, his misplaced loyalty had been cruelly exposed. As he'd worked with one practised eye trained on the boiler; he had inadvertently started an auxiliary pump and increased the cooling water pressure on the main engine by a factor of two. Something had had to give, in this case it had been a spring loaded relief valve situated at engine-room floor plate level. As a fierce jet of water had risen viciously up through the engine-room skylight and sprayed the foredeck; Frank, in the belief that the old tub had

71

been holed, had acted instinctively. He had rung, 'Stop Engines' on the telegraph, to warn the Bridge Officer of his intention; and then swiftly wound back the levers that would bring the huge engine to a shuddering halt.

When any ship, for whatever reason, has lost her means of propulsion at sea, the rules and procedures are manifestly clear. She must immediately display two large black balls at her masthead, this to warn encroaching vessels. As the old *Celtic Trader* had slowly but surely began to lose way; the third mate hastily recruited some deck hands, but the search for the necessary black balls had drawn a noisy and frustrated blank.

Meanwhile, down in the engine-room, the chief and second engineer finally sorted out Frank Kelly's problems. As, with bridge permission, they re-started the prime mover; the deck crew had then relinquished their fruitless search, amid very audible allegations that 'the old cow had no bloody balls!' After a hastily convened get together, Captain McLean and George Venn, the chief engineer, decided to call the whole messy incident a techno-logical stalemate. A phyrric draw no less, an incident which would not bear logging in the voyage log book.

The huge towering old ore carrier, sailing light ship, had picked up way once more and continued to travel southwards, the russet stains of many a sea battle showing on her grey hull. They arrived at last, without further trauma and on kindly seas, at the North African Port for which they were destined. The old *Celtic Trader*, despite the unexpected pause on the voyage, had averaged a creditable twelve knots over the outward leg from Glasgow.

The loading of the *Celtic Trader* had commenced almost immediately, taking place in an atmosphere of sullen resentment. It transpired that the country of Mauretania was suffering the painful pangs of yet another aborted coup. When the dockers had finally and expertly completed loading the ore carrier down to, and a mite beyond, her plimsoll line; Captain McLean ordered the immediate closing of all deck hatches. The crew then began to hose down the main deck. Within forty-eight hours, and studiously ignoring adverse weather reports, the sluggish, heavy laden old vessel had been finally made shipshape, turned around, and coaxed back out into the now threatening Atlantic swell.

Now, two days out from Mauretania, and fighting heavy seas on her way to her home port; the *Celtic Trader* was suffering the wrath of the Bay of Biscay at its worst. For the umpteenth time she lurched sluggishly to port, then buried her forecastle deep down into the grey green depths of the Atlantic Ocean. As she tried to right herself, she shuddered noisily from bow to stern, and for a long long moment she seemed reluctant to free her battered hull from the lethal embrace of the stormy waters.

Jones, the third mate, as he watched his huge ship slowly and reluctantly start to release herself from the sea's terrible embrace, whispered anxiously on the moonlit bridge.

"Come up you old cow!"

That was the trouble with ore carriers, something like 80% of the cargo would be discarded as waste product in the steelworks smelting process when they eventually reached port. Skippers, aware of this high waste factor, tended to load the carriers down to their lines, and sometimes beyond, if the truth were known; to compensate for the massive percentage of waste product that was being shipped.

It was a cute little deception really. At Mauretania they had loaded her down to the Atlantic plimsoll line, and then on down to a couple of inches beyond it. On the seven day voyage back to the Hartlepool ore terminal they would burn off a few hundred tons of fuel oil in her huge six cylinder Doxford opposed piston diesel engine. This would have a positive lightening effect; add to this fresh water used, and by the time they arrived at home port she would have buoyed herself back to her legal draught. A neatly worked and profitable little deception. But, on reflection not really so clever when, like tonight, the old tub had to ply its trade in the Bay of Biscay in a seething force ten gale.

The third mate edged his way slowly across the heaving bridge to where the Quartermaster was jockeying the steering wheel.

"How is she steering Mr Smythe?" The question had been asked with studied casualness as he checked the compass bearing.

"Steering like a pig third mate! She just doesn't want to hold a

73

d

straight course. I'm fighting a helluva yaw to port; if this storm doesn't ease a bit, and pronto, the wife might soon be drawing my company pension."

It was the nearest that Jimmy Smythe, the tough Glaswegian Quartermaster, would get to admitting his fear.

Jones grunted agreement and then moved, with forced calm, back towards the chart-room; all the time wondering desperately whether he should give the skipper a shake. It was now two in the morning though; the old man might not see the funny side! With thoughts of a 'bad discharge' report, he decided that he'd better literally hang on till the end of his watch. His decision made, he began to dream about that lorry driver's job that he'd been offered back home in Shropshire during his previous leave. Being young and low in imagination however, his pessimism was quickly vanishing.

The *Celtic Trader* shuddered along the whole length of her massive bulk, veered uncontrollably to port and tried to bury her rusty structure once more beneath the crashing, spray lashed waves. Her ore filled holds, holds big enough when empty to have allowed the crew to play football matches in on the outward leg of her journey; were now attempting to drag her down, down. Down to that point where she was almost, but not quite, making a lie of every principle ever expounded by the late and oft lamented archimedes. Jones, clinging on with barely concealed panic, had just decided to wake the skipper, come what might, when McLean, to his utter and barely stifled relief, appeared beside him; having hauled himself with surprising alacrity up the companionway from his warm cabin. The captain, a Stornoway man who'd spent at least forty of his fifty-odd years messing about in boats of one kind or another. Uttered a brief, "Morning third mate, she seems to be suffering a wee bit!"

Before Norman Jones could frame a reply he moved nimbly over to study the compound clinometer; mounted midships, just above the Quartermaster's head. For all of three minutes he studied the instrument as it aped faithfully the demented movements of the distressed old ore carrier. Then; his mind made up, he reached out for the bridge phone which would connect him to the cabin of George Venn, the ship's ancient but nevertheless still redoubtable chief engineer.

When he eventually made contact, the chief's gruff voice betrayed no annoyance whatever at the skipper's abrupt intrusion into his slumbers. In times of crisis at sea, there were no such things as eight hour days.

McLean, speaking in a soft but authoritative lilt, wasted no time in inane pleasantries.

"Yes, it's me chief! Now at the last sounding of the port No. 3 double bottom tank we discovered that you had 500 tons of gash fuel oil up your sleeve. Does that situation still pertain?"

Venn must have given him an affirmative; for he raced on.

"Right then, I realise it's your little emergency nest egg that the company knows nothing about. But times are now serious, we'll have to lighten, and I mean lighten, this ship right now; and especially on the port side. Could be a matter of life and death, like yours and mine for starters; so I want it pumped overboard. Frig the bird life, and the same to the environmentalists, we've a ship to save. And, by the way, could I have constant bilge pumping? What's you fresh water situation? Do we really need 400 tons of fresh water just to cool your engine chief? No? Right then, pump 300 tons overboard; this old lady is screaming for buoyancy. Better to be safe and thirsty than end up drinking salt water in the close company of the bloody fish population.

After ending with a less formal "Ciao!" the skipper hung up, studied the clinometer, and listened for a moment to the tortured, agonised groans emanating from the bowels of his old ship. No, now was most definitely not the right time to inform the crew that the old *Celtic Trader's* sister ship had bought oblivion three months back. Having disappeared with all hands, in a heavy laden condition, as she had fought a typhoon off Japan. Turning to the third mate, McLean remarked in a calm and reassuring voice.

"You're doing fine Mr Mate – steady as she goes! Reduce the revs if things deteriorate, and drop in and give me a report when you leave the bridge at four. Our little tinkerings should have begun to have some effect by then."

As Jones, reassured, nodded a friendly reply; the skipper

turned and disappeared down the companionway from which he'd come. Smythe, still jockeying the steering wheel, muttered audibly, "Christ, what a frigging man!"

Norman Jones, hearing the quartermaster's unsolicited commendation, retorted in his turn.

"Amen to that Jimmy Boy! Amen to that!"

Down in the hot and cacophonic engine room, the chief engineer's instructions had reached Frank Kelly, the fourth engineer, via the intercom. Frank, now ever alert for trouble, was scanning the gauges and the huge upper opposed pistons of the gleaming Doxford diesel engine with a practised eye. He knew the main primary mover and her attendant auxiliaries every mood. But now, as the ship's stern lifted at intervals from the water, and her prop threshed the air; the aspinall governor would cut in momentarily and stop the engine. There would be that long agonising moment of silence before the engine would pick up again, with its re-assuring roar and thunderous power. But if at some future moment, especially in the weather they were now experiencing, the engine failed to cut in and pick up again; then the proverbial shit would, most assuredly, hit the fan.

After chatting momentarily with the donkeyman, the fourth engineer once more checked the cooling water gauges, then methodically began to implement the chief's relayed instructions. He fed steam from the engine exhaust boiler into the reciprocating bilge pump and opened the valve which led to the shaft tunnel strum box, where the prop shaft leakage collected. He then deftly repeated the operation, this time bringing the fuel oil transfer pump into play, he next opened the valve which led to the chief's purloined oil in the number three port bottoms; all that was left then was the skin valve which would exit the oil into the raging sea, reluctantly he turned the wheel which would open this.

Such environmental vandalism was wholly against Frank's natural instincts. But the chief would not have decided on this modus operandi without thought. He didn't usually just throw overboard such a valuable oil hoard 'just what would his Greenpeace wife and her friends think of him?' Coming to the

76

conclusion that they would certainly not be amused; Frank, totally at ease amid the cacophony, hum and controlled turmoil; then turned his attention to the problem of dumping 300 tons of precious fresh water overboard.

By the time eight bells signalled the end of his 4am watch, the bilges had been pumped out, and the chief's precious surplus oil had been dumped out into the tumultuous night seas; it would have already emulsified, thus escaping the gaze of any over-flying pilot. Meanwhile the fresh water, the life-line of both ship and crew, was still being pumped out, all the while being constantly monitored by the chippy.

As Frank was meticulously recording the various watch activities in the engine room log book, this for the second engineer's guidance when he handed over. Up on the bridge, Jones was noting in his log that the huge ship was less distressed. the *Celtic Trader* was now at last responding well, and riding more comfortably on the turbulent waves. Captain McLean's initiations seemed to have solved some of the ship's immediate problems.

Round about seven that morning, a little bit of excitement developed on the four to eight watch. The QE2, limping southward on her maiden voyage, was having world publicised problems with her malfunctioning main turbines. As she passed slowly along the starboard side of the *Celtic Trader*, Frank Bell, the Scottish second officer of the rusty old ore carrier, never one to miss an opportunity, lifted the aldis. He then signalled smilingly across to the bridge crew of the beautifully majestic, but incongruously suffering giant.

"What ship? Where bound? Can we be of assistance?"

As the whole of civilisation knew by that time that she was on a thank you voyage to the Canaries; limping along with a load of shipbuilders and other assorted dignitaries; Frank Bell's mock solicitous query must have seemed to her bridge officers to be at best very funny, and at worst decidedly impudent. But the coin came down funny side up, for their return signal of acknow-ledgement, though brief, was equally pithy.

"QE2 – Canaries bound – thanks, but no thanks, not yet that

desperate! Best regards and bon voyage . . ."

The short but historic exchange would be a story which many of the *Celtic Trader's* crew would recall and dine off for many a year to come.

Further excitement was to ensue when it was suddenly discovered that the ship had run out of fresh water. Following on, on the four to eight watch, the second engineer had trusted too implicitly the chippy's fresh water tank soundings in such tumultuous seas. As a result he let the overboard discharge of the precious commodity overrun — with now disastrous results. But as his wife was on board this trip, and the storm was making true soundings an almost impossible exercise; the tragic circumstances were a wee bit too nebulous to pin blame on any one individual. Sure, the seas were now going down a bit, but the main engine still needed a constant top up of fresh cooling water; as did the engine exhaust boiler and the galley, not forgetting the crew.

Another hastily convened ad-hoc meeting between a flustered Captain McLean and George Venn the chief engineer, resulted in much suppressed agitation and inspired calculating, before a workable solution was eventually agreed upon. The ship's messy old emergency evaporator, if run properly, could convert enough sea water to accommodate the main engines cooling requirements. The engine exhaust boiler could tick over, for the few days needed, on sea water input; its annual inspection, soon due, would clean out any salt residues. That left the crew and the galley staff. After a quick check in his maritime regulations manual, and a brief word with the chief engineer, the skipper picked up the tannoy microphone and announced.

"Now hear this, this is your Captain speaking; we have developed a fresh water problem. We are four days out from Hartlepool and our fresh water supply has bottomed. As from now, all crew will be furnished with six cans of lager each day by the ship's chief steward. This may be used for drinking or dhobi. Either way, no man will turn up on watch in a pissed condition, or I'll have him under regulation 14, is this understood? End of message."

As the crew took in the announcement, their eyes brightened perceptibly. They'd never heard of Regulation 14 before, but who the hell cared? Things were at last looking up on the old *Celtic Trader*. Sometime later, down in the galley, McLean was reassured by the chief steward that many a sumptuous repast could, and would be constructed, using lager as a base ingredient; once more a potentially grave crisis had been swiftly and amicably averted.

The following afternoon however, on the noon to four watch, Frank Kelly found himself once again in the throes of crisis. Bad luck seemed to be following the old ore carrier, and yet again, he found himself in the thick of the swiftly developing drama. The donkeyman had been routinely changing boiler fuel burners. He switched on the fuel pump and ignited the burner. Only to discover too late that the newly fitted burner nozzle had been assembled in reverse position. A gush of flaming oil spewed, not into the boiler, but outwards, landing on the tank tops situated below the floor plates, where it immediately began to burn at an alarming and ever increasing rate.

Frank quickly shut down the fuel pump and banged the alarm button to alert the chief. He then grabbed an extinguisher from the very contrite donkeyman. Together they lifted the floor plates, dropped onto the tank tops and began desperately to attack the eagerly spreading flames. Hampered as they were by both pipelines and bulkheads, their task proved to be both difficult and dangerous; this especially when they crawled under the bedplate of the huge, thundering engine. But by the time the chief and the other off watch engineers had finally scrambled down to their aid, the flames had been brought under control and extinguished.

When eventually Captain McLean reached the scene, the causal events were carefully recounted, all pertinent questions being truthfully answered by the donkeyman. Frank, sweating and smoke blackened, expecting to be lauded like some latter day hero for saving the old ship in her moment of distress; met with a wholly unexpected reaction. The skipper and the chief ushered him down to the comparative quiet of the prop shaft tunnel. When he then spoke, the Captain's voice was pitched just higher than the rolling, thundering hum of the prop shaft. "It was a fine job you did out there fourth engineer! A great damage limitation exercise, heroic stuff! But having said all that, it isn't something we would want to go public on now, would we? You're an intelligent young engineer, with a good future ahead of you. Your mess bill says you're sober inclined, well, most of the time." McLean's searching eyes laughingly met Franks. Frank, remembering the two bottles of whisky, guiltily tore his gaze away, the skipper must have known his part in the outward bound incident all the time. Unfazed, McLean continued where he'd left off.

"Marine insurance tend to want to punish shipping companies which allow fires to light, however accidentally in the engine rooms of their ships. If they get to hear about such fires that is! Do you think that on this occasion you could forego the medals and handle the silence? For the good of the company, of course?"

Frank gazed momentarily into McLean's almost innocent blue eyes, glanced towards the stoic, star gazing, chief; and heard himself answer, almost proudly.

"No problem Captain, whichever way you want to play it! I can only answer for myself of course. But you and the chief here can regard the fire; after we've cleaned up of course; as being a closed chapter, finito!"

He seemed to have spoken wisely, for the relieved smiles of the older men were now reflected in his almost innocent, enquiring gaze. Thus ended Frank's moment of incipient glory.

In the days that followed, nothing more occurred to shatter the tense, uneasy peace. And they eventually limped, at half revolutions, to save the engine from overheating, into the outer harbour at Hartlepool. The *Celtic Trader* was drawing too much water to safely cross the sand-bar which protected the inner harbour, so they noisily dropped anchor and awaited events.

Purely on a personal level, over the final three days sailing, there had been the odd little niggle. But the beer ration had ensured that the run into port could best be described as having taken place in an alcohol induced environment of high spirits. All this under the threatening but futile glare of the skipper and his fellow officers. A brief highlight of the run in had occurred when the second engineer's wife had been observed by a steward running along the alleyway from the heads brandishing a pair of pink knickers. It later transpired that while daydreaming in the loo, the sense that she was not alone was abruptly confirmed when the wet nose of a swimming rat had come momentarily into contact with a briefly exposed part of her nether anatomy. The reality of fleas and cockroaches she had managed to endure on the voyage; but for her, rats proved to be the final straw! The hilarious incident had put the second engineer's problem with the fresh water, or lack of it, into its true perspective.

As he finally came alongside the wallowing *Celtic Trader*, the company's shipping agent was the unwitting harbinger of bad news. As they were still drawing far too much water, it would be another four days at least before favourable tidal conditions would allow the old ore carrier to cross the sand-bar; and be then coaxed into the safety of the discharge berth in the inner harbour. McLean casually enquired as to the cost of bringing out a fresh water tender; without of course mentioning their present little water crisis. He had long ago learned that in the company of shipping agents, some things were best left unsaid. As the agent quoted the present cost of offshore water tendering, McLean pursed his lips in disbelief. No way would the company let such an expense occur without forwarding to the skipper the inevitable, 'We fail to understand . . .' letter. The die was now cast, his crew were condemned to survive on lager till they eventually got alongside. A situation which as yet none of them had shown any signs of challenging.

Despite the incredibly fragile condition of her crew, the old cow was finally nudged into port by two attendant tugs, her prop clanking out a melody from her bobbing beer can wake. Less than an hour later, as the skipper watched from the bridge, some of the crew began to noisily and cheerfully troop down the gangway. They would be heading through the dock sheds to the nearby railway station and their train home to Glasgow.

"Ay, enjoy your leave lads!" He whispered bitterly as he gazed down. He had been informed by the agent that the shipping company were about to flog the *Celtic Trader* to Greek factors. There, underpaid and less professional crews, working to lower safety margins under a flag of convenience, the latter to reduce insurance premiums; might, just might, bolster presently unpredictable profit margins. He'd checked the agents story of course, the company under manager proving to be aggressively forthright when he'd answered the phone.

"Please understand Captain McLean! UK crews are proving to be too expensive. Too much trade unionism! Ridiculous sick leave and safety costs! Insurance margins and repair bills! Need we go on?"

They didn't have to, he had hung up in disgust. They had given no thought to, or even mentioned, that most of the crew he'd just sailed triumphantly through bad times with were soon to be literally washed up; beached! On the proverbial frigging rocks! Just a few more burdens on an increasingly fragile state.

That evening, to the noisy background of Stevedores unloading iron ore, he dined in the officer's mess with the chief engineer. After listening at length to McLean's woes, Venn, a dour Glaswegian, butted in.

"You're not reading the runes very well, Mac! Can't you see that steel-making, shipping, mining and the smoke stack industries in Britain are ripe candidates for dodoville? Just as pack roads, canals and even railways have fallen to the more flexible lures of road and air transport; so also is our age of steel, our particular world; giving way to the joys of plastic living. What we can't make competitively now, we can buy in from the cheap labour industries round the Pacific rim for half the price. In Parliament the other day they were lauding our city whiz kids, who had wrought the modern economic miracle of making money without working for it. Money itself is now the product. We've put the middle man, and his sweat, into the dole queue. New technology rules skipper!"

As Venn paused and prepared another glass of whisky to slake his thirst, McLean leaned across the mess table and asked pointedly.

"OK Chief, what's the answer? What's the bloody answer?"

The Chief laid down his drink and gazed quizzically over at the skipper.

"The answer my friend, as the old song says, is blowing in the wind. We must throw away the oily rag and make sure our next generation can talk computers and electronics. That way they can then be ready to serve the new technologies. They're coming fast from the Far East; Pearl Harbour and the River Kwai are history, and why not? Today we must dance to the tune of a new synergy."

The Chief paused momentarily, then continued, "As for you skipper, you'll never be out of work! Round the globe there are shipping companies looking for men like yourself. Men who can overcome adverse conditions, lead men wisely, and bring home safely tired old buckets like the *Celtic Trader* here. Me? I'll sink into the sunset with the old red duster!"

"Is this really your last voyage Chief?" McLean's voice, as he asked the question, betrayed a genuine concern. "I can't really see you putting your feet up back there in Glasgow!"

"Hold on Mac! Who mentioned Glasgow, there's nothing back there at the moment except a burnt out husk of industrial revolution, and I haven't yet mentioned the buildings. No; Hurrah for the joys of the housing recession. The wife and I have bought a wee small holding down near Weymouth. A bungalow with six acres. You're now looking at a farmer who is about to become an expert in his own field! Thank God, no more bloody water shortages!"

"Water shortages Chief? by the looks of that carafe you're diluting your whisky with, some of us have suffered greater water shortages than others!"

"Maybe so Captain, but don't forget that it was my illegal little oil well that saved your ship!"

Smiling at the Chief's riposte, the Captain reluctantly left the mess to go and supervise the imminent loading of fresh water. On his way he suddenly remembered and deviated to the bridge to write up his end of voyage log. This last voyage would require some very carefully scripted annotation. He looked back over the log to previous entries. The last three voyages had ended with the innocuous descriptive conclusion, 'voyage uneventful'. After this last few weeks of nautical mayhem and personal stress however, such a stilted concluding description could no longer pertain. He had better, on this occasion, be less uncompromising. One had to foresee, and be prepared to combat, the possibility of future repercussions.

McLean took up his old ball point pen and never one to make a drama out of the odd crisis, wrote clearly and neatly in the voyage summary remarks column: 'Voyage comparatively uneventful.'

12
And On the Third Day . . .

In his cold, sparse, Islington flat, a shivering Steve Devlin scanned his Monday morning mail, groaned and scratched his russet locks in consternation. How had it happened? How the hell could he have come to make such a basic error? Some arranger of rallies he'd turned out to be! Talk about losing his touch! Again he keenly scanned the contents of the cold, concise letter.

'. . . we fail to understand why you booked some 28 members of the Royal Society for the Protection of Birds onto an excursion coach bound for a Cats' Protection League Rally at Birmingham Exhibition Centre? This must surely be some sort of a . . ?'

Steve threw the wounding letter down in consternation. He would have to save this one till later. Right now more pressing problems were vying for his entrepreneurial skills. But bird nuts travelling all that way to join a cat party! His amused smile metamorphosed momentarily the virtues of reality. It was enough, he decided, to make organic gardeners till it like it was! OK, so he'd made one mistake last week, but it hadn't all been bad news! Hadn't he led a headline grabbing attack on the government's water privatisation fiasco? Not forgetting either the loud, but successful, defence of men's equality in matters of pensions and prescription charges? True, 'Mental Handicap in the Community' had bombed. But in this business, there was no way you were going to win them all, that was for sure. He needed this criticising letter like he needed the proverbial hole in the head. Parodying the trees which grew in the local Lovers' Lane, he now most definitely felt much more sinned against than sinning.

Steve consulted his grubby diary. At three this afternoon he would support an organised protest in Hyde Park, a 'Troops out of Northern Ireland' march. Like Noel Coward, he harboured a talent to abuse. He readied his tools and materials and began thoughtfully to plan his banner for the day's work.

There, finished at last! He fixed the stark message onto a brush pole, and paused to admire his handiwork. That would shake the bloody imperialists. The message read starkly, in bold black letters 'Implantation to Paisley! Partition without democracy! Time now to go, colonial foe!' There! That would show them, that would rouse the abominable 'no' men of Whitehall. Though in retrospect the banners historical references would in all probability be beyond the ken of their public school intellect.

As he strolled towards the incipient demo, Steve pointedly ignored the studied, sometimes baleful, glares of the passing populace as they caught a glimpse of his shouldered message. He was becoming acutely aware that, in these heady post-Thatcherite days, soldiers and policemen were not quite so hampered anymore by the constraints of an increasingly flexible rule of law. These were serious accusations, but past evidence of 'State Assassination Services' in Gibraltar, coupled to Stalker's experiences in Northern Ireland, had lowered Britain's legal system to banana republic level. At least that was his view of it! Steve tightened his by now sweaty grasp on the brush handle and strode gamely forward. He was edgy but who the hell needed a life of compromise! As Christ may have once said, "No pain, no gain"! Parliament would sooner or later have to realise that if you give a starving man a laxative, all you'll get back is the laxative.

He reached the milling 'Troops Out' procession at last and joined it with his banner proudly raised. Beside him a pensioner was shuffling along on legs which were manifestly unfit for the task. As he gave the old man a friendly arm, he noted with some surprise that he was proudly wearing a VC, which was dangling from a faded ribbon. Talk about a dichotomy! Steve's moment of cognitive dissonance quickly passed, however. Hadn't, in retrospect, some seventy thousand southern Irishmen fought alongside British comrades in World War Two? It was now obvious that they hadn't all been cowards. Even if Eire's stubborn neutrality in 1939 had disdained Britain's carrot of a United Ireland – if the historians were to be believed that was – but as the man once said "there was really no future in history"! And this procession of protest, though puny, was at least better late than never.

As they shuffled forward, there was a brief moment of confusion when they converged momentarily with a more sedate group touting the vain glorious advantages of female priesthood. Before Steve, who had strong views on this one, could get close enough to direct a well aimed raspberry in their direction, the police had sorted out the problem.

Some minutes later his reverie was abruptly interrupted by a loud Ulster voice shouting from the pavement edge.

"Ye're all on our list! Ye Irish shits!"

Again Steve failed to react, though he could well understand what the guy was going through. Given the prevailing political circumstances, he was bound to be edgy.

The shuffling procession having reached Downing Street at last, in a brief moment of anticlimax the handing in of the 'Troops Out' petition proved to be a solemn but low key moment in the proceedings. Steve then left his banner propped against a convenient wall and headed for the nearest ale house.

He had barely downed his first mouthful when a well soused gent with an, 'I drink, therefore I am,' countenance sidled over, nudged him, and said gloatingly, "What about that lot then! The friggin' communists have folded. Their regime's collapsed like a pack of bloody cards. So much for the philosophy of Stalin, Gorbachov and that ilk, pal. Give me good old fashioned capitalism every time!"

Steve, remembering the string of cheats and fraudsters who had weaselled their way in and out of the English courts over the last decade or so, all under the benevolent banner of a capitalism reflecting man's inhumanity to man, buried his tongue in his pint and deemed it better not to reply. Instead, he drained his glass, nodded sagely and bade the guy a saccharin farewell. Who wanted to objectively discuss politics with someone whose thinking was somewhere to the right of Genghis Khan?

After his escape, he was walking past Trafalgar Square, on his way home, when he heard the chants and cries of anguish emanating from that popular place of democratic outrage. Presupposing police brutality, Steve, sidling in for a closer look, found himself crouching in the shadow of a recumbent lion, from which vantage point he surveyed the clamorous scene. He might have guessed it! Just another bunch of assorted Zionists, all furiously protesting the military posturing of Iraq's Saddam Hussein. Their banners screamed it all: 'No democracy in Iraq!' 'Saddam must go!' and 'Stop Iraq's Atomic Bombs!' As the Israeli sympathisers noisily resisted police pressure, Steve, dragging a lump of chalk from the capacious pocket of his flak jacket, began to print swiftly on the lion's plinth, in bold, cultured, italic writing.

"Remember Vanunu! You Yankee lackeys!"

He had just completed his defiant riposte, written with the aim of democratic balance, when the retreating protesters, fleeing from what a sympathetic press would tomorrow no doubt call 'Police brutality', turned towards Steve in their panic. They just couldn't miss his stark message. Enraged, they made purposefully towards where he was standing, chalk still in hand, and the turd now touching the cloth! Not one to mess about in such adverse circumstances, Steve bolted. As he made his escape, his thoughts raced ahead of him. Typical bloody Jews! Coupled the holocaust to the collective conscience of the West as a lever to steal Palestine from the Arabs. Anyone who dared to protest was branded as being an anti-Semite! Nice little ploy that one. No wonder they chose Barrabas way back then!

Steve bolted down a side street and paused momentarily for breath. He would have to stop panicking, get his act together; first things first, that was it! He went to the Post Office and collected his benefit before making his way home to his old run-down flat once more.

Home at last, he made a cup of tea, then began to work through his protest schedule for the coming week. As he rifled through his old diary, his eyes began to glisten with hardly suppressed glee. It looked as though he was going to have a few interesting days ahead of him this coming week after all.

Tomorrow he would have to gear himself up to heckle the Gay Rights March scheduled for eleven o'clock. A tricky assignment that would be, for they were increasingly insinuating the support of some intellectual 'luvvies', not forgetting the odd titled roué. But despite their up front persuasions in politics and the media, the ugh factor still showed through. Morality aside, if they didn't recognise the natural function of the sex act, that meant they were stupid. And if they did know, and continued to try to impregnate turds, then that made them perverse. Of course some queers were only in it for money or influence.

Either way, they and their cousins the paedophiles, were paying dearly for their vicarious pleasures. Steve decided that his banner must also mention fisting, faeces eating, rough trade, Bangkok and the dilution of the English language, before he moved on to the following day's business.

Ah yes! Wednesday morning would resurrect the old argument about when a foetus was not and when it was a child; a sensitive subject that, especially with his sister Viv's present condition. A careful handling of this one was undoubtedly called for. Less subtlety would, of course, be required at Friday night's confrontation with the National Front. Their 'No more immigrants' bash, up the East End, was sure to become a fricative experience, for last time they had clashed, he had been lucky to escape with a partially kicked in head. As Steve at last tidied up his desk for the night, the news reader on the TV was revealing the latest beneficiaries of the National Lottery. Bloody hell! Wasn't it now becoming more and more obvious that the have nots were being milked to support the recreations of the upper classes. As the old song said: 'When will they ever learn?'

Night was falling as he left the flat in search of a take-away pizza. One second normality, with thoughts of melting cheese and ham, and the next the awful searing explosion in his head. As the pain shot through his whole being, a fleeting expression of triumph, almost of victory, wreathed his suffering countenance.

He had subconsciously lived his life in the hope of dying nobly for a cause. Was this the moment then? Almost immediately his expression changed to one of abject puzzlement. It seemed that he'd got his wish, his martyrdom. But what cause? What frigging cause was he now about to lay down his restless life for? With this last question sadly still unanswered, his handsome face lost all sign of life and he lay oh so still, by now utterly oblivious of the human clamour that cosseted his bleeding, prostrate body. A mounting cacophony which prefaced the arrival of a hastily summoned ambulance.

Under the concentrated lighting of the hot, muggy operating theatre, Dr Findley worked swiftly and methodically. As his skilled fingers probed deftly in the skull region of the prostrate Steve, his every move and thought process was being relayed, through a small clip-on microphone, to the three students ensconced in the viewing gallery. Speaking in a soft but firm Highland lilt, he began.

"The patient is now comfortable under sedation and on oxygen, gentlemen, a very important first step that. Here we have a typical, falling slate induced example, of an upper cranial puncture, with brain damage complications. Having cleaned and shaved the area of penetration, we drill the puncture and finish up with a neat round hole in the plate; remembering, of course, not to carelessly lose any bone fragments therein. We now insert the vacuum equipment to remove any clotting material and hope that the contusions on the brain surface will eventually heal. Either way, only time and intensive care will tell. The clotting materials removed, we close the drilled aperture with this plastic snap-in press stud. A permanent silver plate will, of course, be provided when future X-rays reveal a satisfactory conclusion to our efforts. To pre-empt some of your questions, yes, there will be some occasional pain in the cortex region for a considerable time post op, but this we can control with phased injections of pyro-tebbitine. In many cases of cranial puncture such as this one, there has been some evidence of a marked personality shift. But always remember that everything, when compared with death, is relative; this includes the aforementioned possibility of personality disorder."

After three days, Steve rose again from the bed, his head throbbing; he then began to survey his sterile environment. Try as he did, his memory of the past was, alas, in malfunction mode. Without retrospect, the past had become another country. As his soup diet was gradually replaced by solids, the old man in the next bed kindly began to feed his anxious intellect by handing him each day copies of the *Sun* and *Telegraph* newspapers. He listened avidly to radio and, bit by bit, he began to reformulate some sort of plan, a philosophy even, for his future existence. It would not be easy but . . . A few days later, as promised, the Doctor proudly snapped the silver plate onto his exposed skull. The ugly reminders they then covered with a cute little peakless skull cap. Steve, as he caught sight of his reconstituted image, smiled uneasily.

When he at last left the hospital, his first faltering steps were interrupted by a grubby, aggressive member of London's homeless community, who demanded loutishly, "How's about a couple of quid for my bed, guv?"

Steve, driven to riposte, answered skittishly, "I'd need to see it first mate! And anyway, I don't really need one right now!"

When he eventually reached his flat, a cursory examination of the piles of radical rubbish filed around the living space almost turned his stomach. In came a dozen black plastic bags and out in them went the almost complete totality of his reckless past. He then tentatively approached Joe Goldstein, his landlord, with a view to extracting a modicum of compensation for the offending slate. The latter, however, vociferously denied all responsibility for Steve's untimely accident, all the while proclaiming that it had been an 'Act of God'. Steve left wondering just which God had acted on Goldstein's behalf, deciding eventually to let the claim drop. He had much more pressing problems to occupy his confused and painful mind.

He discovered that Social Security payments were now being coupled to relevant training courses. He had to eat, so he opted for a full time course in Computer Studies, this coupled to Chartered Accountancy. Two years' later, amid cries of "Brilliant!" he had graduated. He was then head-hunted by a major insurance company in London, at their pipe-fitter's nightmare HQ, and took up the position of Assistant Claims Assessor. Steve then astutely took out a mortgage and moved to an admittedly dank, steamy, basement flat in Cadogen Square; for, after all, if you lived in London, it was assuredly your postcode and address that shaped your future.

Round about then, Jinny moved into his life, a third string Government researcher at that point in time; she was a much sought after darling of the Hampshire hunting fraternity. A lucky man, times were at last really looking up for him! The rumour of promotion soon insinuated itself and there was even more good news emanating from the benevolent insurance company pipeline. He was asked casually one lunch-time over beer and sandwiches if he'd like an introduction to the delightful Diana at the next Exchange Ball? He spluttered into his *Financial Times* with uncontrolled pride. Things were indeed on the move and the direction was ever upwards.

Right then though, remembering heads, the pain in his cortex was still recurring; admittedly at an ever diminishing rate. At times his brain seemed to be uneasy, to be probing futilely at the shroud which seemed to have enveloped his memory of the now long past. Though such searching brought on the pain, he always found relief in Doctor Findley's cortex injections. Despite the rising costs, a further injection of pyro-tebbitine from the good Doctor's medicine cabinet, painless and over in seconds, made him feel 'all right' again. A feeling that now stayed with him for literally months at a time.

Passing events in the real world proved to be the ultimate gauge of Steve's progressing development. He wept buckets for the lost genius of such greats as Freddie Mercury and Kenny Everett when they had predictably cashed in their proverbial cheques. And when Private Lee Clegg hit the streets, a free man again, Steve, with Jinny in Fuengirola at the time, had rushed vociferously to verbally defend the challenged decision. These being the natural reactions, one would contend, of a man who, purely coincidentally, happened to have a hole in his head.

13

Terminus

In an attempt to compensate the weary overnight train travellers for the long night of drifting snow stoppages, the station buffet manager had enterprisingly laid on a cheap breakfast of bangers and egg at forty-seven pence. As the intercity express from London had just disgorged more than a hundred hungry passengers who would have to wait another two hours for their North Highland connection, business at the self-service counter of the station cafeteria was, to understate the case, brisk. It was a motley queue; blinking reactor bound atomic scientists and loud American technicians, the latter group north bound for the tracking station, rubbed shoulders with a sprinkling of multi-coloured skiers and a contingent of young soldiers. The soldiers, about fifty of them, sporting Green Howard flashes, were on route to winter training in the snow clad mountains. Here, in the cafeteria, they were meeting up with a similar number of their comrades in arms, who, their hill training completed, were due to take the newly arrived express back south, but that would not be until the cleaning and refuelling staffs had completed their routine chores.

In the noisy atmosphere of such a socio-cultural intermix, it was not surprising that the boisterous interchanges of the young soldiers began to dominate. How was the camp accommodation? The grub? Was the course difficult? Any local birds? Did they lay? Like a hectic game of verbal ping pong, questions chased answers all round Joe as he sat in his usual corner seat, his big hands cradling a cup of hot, but indifferent quality, railway tea. In spite of the years which had presented him with his steel grey hair and peering eyes, the noisy scene reminded him forcibly of his own stint in the navy. They had been happy times too! And hadn't he been at an age then when all the girls in his world had been excitingly bad and made to be had?

Ah yes? hadn't they been the hock cock days! A period during which he'd lugged a blanket, ever at the ready, on top of his holdall, and it hadn't been for warmth either. That blanket could have been the source of a few stories, but today they'd never get past Mary Whitehouse. However, that had been a very long yesterday ago. Today, here he was, mechanic at a logging camp, drifting into the city on Saturday mornings to see who was coming in off the London train. Big deal twilight! However, he usually picked up a few second-hand anecdotes with which to regale the lads back at the lumber yards.

His cup empty for the second time, Joe rejoined the noisy self-service queue for a refill. In the shuffling procession towards the spitting tea urn he watched with mounting blood pressure as a young soldier with laden tray made purposefully for his temporarily vacated corner seat.

"Damn these transients!"

But what the hell, there were still some vacant seats over by the door, the floor was slushy over there of course, and it would be much colder . . . but beggars couldn't be choosers, especially in these weather conditions.

As if to emphasise Joe's thoughts, someone momentarily opened the outside door of the Cafeteria. A freezing, snow laden blast rushed into the warm room, causing one young private to shout, "Close that flippin' gate!" It was an involuntary protest echoed by all in the noisy room.

Joe had just left the cash checkout and was making towards the seats by the door, when the old man stumbled desperately in through the storm lashed entrance; looking for all the world like the literal version of the guy who'd come in from the cold, he stumbled over a carelessly discarded back pack and sat down heavily on a vacant seat. Snow cocooned, but too tired to shake himself down, he sat there eyes rolling, his ashen colour emphasised by several days of beard.

He appeared to be just recovering from some just completed task. He looked towards the service counter as though he was expecting a blow. Breathing noisily now, he looked wildly around him at the crowded tables, then slowly, helplessly, a sad, almost apologetic expression on his drawn face, he lowered his head onto his dirty, badly chapped hands and was still. A moment later his cap spilled from his balding grey hair and landed with its cargo of snow on the table.

As Joe approached the empty seat opposite him, the only one left, he studied the still figure. His frayed overcoat carried the traces of a dozen derelict shelters and the blizzard conditions had probably flushed him back into society miles from the old warehouses or brick kilns which were the usual winter haunts of such people. Joe sat down opposite and brushed the snow from the table. Someone had said once that life was lived in three stages, 'I will be!', 'I am!', 'I was!' Joe was in no doubt as to which stage the old man had progressed to. For weeks now the still figure had probably been staving off hypothermia with crutch shots of cheap booze.

Come to think of it, he was lying very still now, almost unnaturally so. Joe impulsively opened his cigarette packet and, leaning over, shook the old man, his fingers sinking into a bony shoulder. "Have a fag old timer, how about a cup of tea? It'll chase the chill!" in response to Joe's gentle shaking the old man's head lolled suddenly, then rolled uncontrollably off his cradling hands, hitting the table with an ominous thud. What had been for Joe an incipient act of charity was now becoming a tragedy. A combination of personal neglect, weather conditions, hunger, social indifference and limp Christianity seemed to have finally turned this derelict into a very dead statistic. He looked as though he would be accepting no more fags from anyone. Trying to control his panic, Joe went round to the old man's side of the table and began to massage the skeletal hands and wrists. The futility of the act had begun to screw up Joe's guts when a voice behind him said gently:

95

"Let me have a try mate, I've done some first aid work!"

Relieved he allowed himself to be pushed aside by one of the colourfully clad skiers. The man began to seek at heart and wrist for signs that the still figure was still in the land of the living. By now the drama had been transmitted round the cafeteria. In the gathering silence, the first-aider paused, moved over to the staring cashier and said authoritatively, "Call the police and an ambulance lass, tell them to get here fast and not to forget the oxygen."

At the mention of oxygen there was a general easing of tension. Oxygen meant that there must be life there for it to feed. Meanwhile the skier had returned to the old man, he shouldered his way through the crowd and looked down at the slumped figure. He thought about applying the kiss of life, changed his mind and began to rub the puny wrists where Joe had left off. Relieved, Joe retired to another empty seat with his cup. The general volume of conversation climbed a few more decibels as the unexpected distraction was now noisily commented upon. As Joe stopped twisting his plastic spoon and reached for another cigarette, an American voice rose momentarily above the general clamour, ". . . a goddam shame, ain't there no contingency plans for. . ." The clamour rose and the soloist was drowned out.

The police beat the ambulance men to the scene. While one ushered back the onlookers the other took up the wrist rubbing and heart massage routine. The area now cleared, the constables paused for a brief consultation over the slumped figure. One of them then extracted a pocket radio. Through the din Joe just managed to pick up the tail-end sentence of a brief conversation with his headquarters ". . . a goner, tell the ambulance men not to kill themselves getting here, over and out."

When the ambulance finally arrived, it drew right into the station forecourt, its flashing blue lights casting ghostly shadows on the driving snow flakes. The doors of the cafeteria burst open and they were wheeling in a low stretcher on top of which was an oxygen bottle. "All this belated attention and the old sod doesn't even know he's getting it!"

Joe overheard the comment, but dismissed it as the front line

96

defence of a confused mind. As the milling crowd watched, the ambulance men made rapid, self assured checks for any signs of life. A despairing shake of the head by one of them brought the audience up with the state of play. He carried the still unused cylinder out to the waiting vehicle. He resumed, then he and his companion, assisted by the two policemen, eased the lifeless bundle onto the stretcher. As they did so an empty wine bottle clattered from among the rags onto the floor. The bottle didn't break. "Another dead man!" mused Joe cynically.

They were now folding the old man's arms across his chest. A grey blanket with red borders was thrown over the still figure and drawn very conclusively up over the ashen grey face. As they began to wheel him out to the storm lashed forecourt one of the skiers lifted the old man's discarded cap, followed them out and placed it gently on his blanket covered breast. It seemed important somehow. A sort of final caring gesture. As Joe watched, a young boy soldier huddled into a corner and was violently sick onto the floor, so much for his first vision of the sharp end of life. But he'd learn, he'd just have to, for wasn't death now his chosen occupation! In no time at all he'd be shamefacedly telling his mocking mates about the bad pint he'd downed on the train.

Soon after the ambulance had screamed off to the mortuary in futile haste. Joe, with time to kill before he left the buffet, ordered a third cup of tea. When he'd finished it, he gathered his old army greatcoat about him and pushed his way purposefully out into the storm. He moved slowly down the street towards the awakening city. It was the only street the old man could have taken on his way to find final warmth at the buffet. Joe noted with some irony that the Citizens' Advice Bureau and the Social Security building were rubbing shoulders a couple of hundred yards from the station, but it was not yet nine, the official crisis solving time, so they were both firmly closed against intrusion. There was a time for a man to die of hypothermia and there was a time for the state to offer succour, a pity they didn't always coincide. The cinema was advertising an old film, *In The Heat of The Night*. Joe smiled, he wondered if the old man had smiled too.

97

While waiting for the pub to open, Joe wandered into the Civic Centre. The building, a modern one, combined Art Gallery, Museum and Library. A hot blast of air-conditioned breeze assailed his pinched face as he opened the swing doors. Plenty of warmth here for the old man. Damn it! He couldn't get the old man out of his mind. Still maybe he'd snuffed it because he couldn't last out to Library opening time. Or, more probably, some little shit of a librarian had shown objection to his unpalatable image on more than one occasion. But who cared anyway! Joe wandered around the non-fiction area, pausing now and then at shelves 'asag' with the philosophies of men long dead. In the gallery there was a display of modem art, but the warm gallery and warmer hues were too much. He skipped the museum altogether and made his way out to the snow-laden street. What good was a civilisation which put warm books and warm colours before warm people? Ban Cruise! Save the Whale! No mileage in the itinerant male. Maybe tomorrow he'd feel different, time would help him to compromise, to come to terms with today's events, but somewhere deep down within him he faintly, savagely, hoped that he never would.

14

The Barnsley Syndrome

Let's face it, Wally was tired of the staid reality that was Barnsley! Bored too of the shelf filling job that had replaced his now defunct career down the pits. Washed up at 47, all he had to look forward to now was probably early death, and an additional small cross down in the cemetery beside his mother and father. The ultimate marker for a person such as himself; for at times his lined face bore the resigned look of someone who was going to be found, not reaching for the proverbial stars, but alone, dead and soon forgotten.

In his many attempts to shuffle off the glooms, Wally became known in his area as 'Super Glue'. He literally joined everything; his pursuits ranging from archery to zinc collecting. His interest in flying started off as being merely an admittedly intense, but nonetheless armchair bound curiosity, in front of the TV. His penurious circumstances precluding any more serious attempts at what might be described as 'hands on' experience. Until he won the forty thousand pounds in the National Lottery that was! It was then that he vacated his armchair, told the supermarket to stuff their own shelves and became an eager student of aeronautics in its wider sense.

In the public library, a brief brush with the mythical exploits of Pegasus and Icarus instilled in his mind the crucial necessity of getting the weight to wingspan correlation just right. And, as for the mistake of flying too near to the sun, modern adhesives would surely overcome such a ridiculous and tragic conclusion to an historic human endeavour. But enough for the moment of the interesting, but ultimately sterile, theory of flight. Real flying was all about being where it was at! Up there, challenging the ether, not just wallowing indolently in the romantic idyll.

His first 'chute drop came about as a result of his eagerly volunteering to represent the local Cancer Charity. Sponsorship was still rolling in that day as he was gently coaxed out of the lumbering old kite at six thousand feet. A wee bit naughtily, he ignored the 'chute opening instruction until he'd rung the ultimate drop of pleasure from the exhilarating joys of free fall flying. Only when he finally noticed that he was about to meet the excited crowd, down below him in the airport, at a closing speed of 120 mph, did he reluctantly decide to activate the rip cord. The resultant gentle jerk on his armpits, followed almost at once by the most wonderful floating feeling he'd ever experienced, confirmed him in his ambition to fly. A confirmation which was not even dented when, a couple of minutes later, he came into abrupt contact with an unforgiving terra firma. As he was proudly and loudly mobbed by his exhilarated sponsors, Wally bit back the pain of an indifferent landing. With regard to flying, he was now, in the parlance of the populace, hooked!

Following on that initial triumph, he soon became not only a parachutist, but also a free fall expert. Even extending his experience into the practical realms of 'flying wing' and hang gliding. He then graduated to towed gliders and microlite machines; but the suffocating close confines of such craft seemed somehow to stifle the raw exhilaration. Not for Wally the noise, the smell or the rigid, structured confines of the closed cockpit. Sure, he wanted to fly, but for real!

Yes, his interest was in real flying, not in the artificially generated variety which necessitated on the one hand noisy smelly engines, or, on the other, high points to launch from; in the hope of attaining some interesting but nevertheless relentless descent. Wally, nursing his disappointment, turned his attentions once more to the theoretical fumblings of the early pioneers.

Da Vinci he decided, had come close to turning human flight theory into hard reality with some of his ideas. But his brilliant concepts had not been matched by the primitive nature of prevailing technology. True, the Gondolfiers had put man up in the clouds, but theirs and Green's hot air balloons had, like Gifford's Airship, done little or nowt to forward the ultimate aim of totally controlled, human actuated flight. Only Otto Lilienthal had kept the dream alive! And as for the Wright Brothers and their contemporaries; their relentless graduation towards power flight had left the human powered flight quest stagnating in the doldrums of aviation history for decades. Of course, to bring it all up to date, there had been that young man who'd pedalled what looked like a plastic bag across the English Channel to France. But with its reliance on cranks and gears, all coupled to brute strength; 'real flying it certainly was not!', concluded Wally.

Now, harbouring a black despair, he returned once more to the comforting embrace of his local free fall group. And he would still have been there today, still awaiting the final ignominy of being planted down in the cemetery by the slag tip; if he hadn't switched on the television one wet evening. David Attenborough was rattling on, in his usual knowledgeable manner about bird flight, when he poured forth what appeared to Wally to be some very fascinating information. It seemed, if he had understood it right, that birds only needed to use power during the downstroke; the wings being then automatically retracted by the wishbone, this in readiness for the next energy sapping downstroke. The wishbone acting magically in the role of a sort of return spring. The information caused a flutter of excitement in the normally placid Wally. It was becoming increasingly obvious to him why little birds could find the energy to tackle inter-continental hops during the migration season. What with single action power strokes, wishbone actuated return strokes and a built in gliding facility; almost any distance, given favourable ambient conditions, was a proverbial dawdle for any half healthy example of the feathered fraternity. But that now took him back full circle to the question he was subconsciously trying to avoid asking himself. 'Could a person, given the optimum weight to wingspan ratio, learn to compete with birds in their lofty environment?'

Could man in essence, with his obviously superior intellect and advanced technological know how, learn to actually fly? Wally, at that specific moment in time, didn't know the answer to his own naively posed question, but he most certainly knew a man who might! His mind now filled with visions of himself having just completed his first solo meander round the globe and the resultant acclaim which would inevitably follow; he headed for the flat wherein lived his old friend Joe.

Joe Inglis was a morose man, a retired engineer whom Wally had conversed with frequently up at the communal allotments. Joe, his many skills now redundant, had felt for some time that he'd early retired into a world of grey anti climax; so it was no surprise that Wally's rambling propositions, shyly but defiantly blurted out; immediately intrigued him. Human powered flight? Gradually but remorselessly the challenging concept was to develop into a series of attainable objectives, all culminating in the ultimate aim; a flying, soaring, gliding, trail blazing Wally.

Over the next few days Joe carefully collected and shaped the required parts. Wally would have to lie prone on a broad, thickly padded board, of about eight feet in length. Two large buggy wheels, fitted across one end would lift the board into a diagonal position. While fitted into the other end would be the small but sturdy, rear wheel. This immediately below the foot operated rudder and ailerons. The very important wishbone effect being ultimately created by hinging a vertical double wishbone onto either side of the base board. The loose arms at the top being married together by joining struts. Some hastily purchased elastic material, laced across the wishbone structure, completed the mechanical arrangement of Wally's Hippogriff.

At this point in production, Wally lay down on the structure, made himself comfortable, gripped the horizontal cross stays of the wishbone and pumped his arms out sideways. The results were immediate and very satisfactory. Each time he pumped, out would go the arms of the wishbone structure; on relaxing, the elastic would bring the arms together against, with a satisfying click, two feet above his head. Pure bloody magic! All that was missing now were the wings. Plastic being agreed upon, and the method of attaching them safely to the upper regions of the wishbone arms worked out, things were indeed progressing apace.

Joe then drew out, and had the fourteen feet wings moulded in the new ultra light diadine plastic at the local extrusion factory. Tapered lengthwise and fore to aft, they were works of art in themselves. They then carefully mounted the wings onto their pre-designed deal supports, before bolting each wing into position on its appropriate wishbone arm. There, almost completed, they now had a human powered bird; but would it fly? Wally positioned himself on the padded baseboard once more and manipulated the wishbone struts; the beautiful yellow wings responded to his every move. Excited now, he savoured the positive vibration as his baby strained to take off. But, how to attain enough height for all their efforts to be viable? They needed something to supply the initial lift which would propel them that hundred or so feet into the air. At which point the beautiful yellow wings should then generate their own lift, drive and stabilised momentum. Joe was to solve this problem in the simplest manner imaginable. As in some long remembered old wooden toy aircraft, he mounted on a bearing a two foot diameter wooden propeller, and clamped it to the forward end of the baseboard. He then hooked the prop' core onto some laced bicycle inner tubes and fed the tubes through an old electrical conduit sling under the base board, it only needed for him to anchor the inner tubes to the rear wheel. He now had a rubber band engine of incalculable power, a few cursory turns of the propeller generated a swift, vicious, but very satisfying reaction. When fully wound, and with a control trigger fitted, they would be more or less ready for the big moment.

The date of launch was preceded by a plethora of detailed instructions. When finally aloft, and comfortable with the machine Wally could jettison the propeller for more positive weight to drag gain and when he eventually attained his 5000 metre ceiling, he could jettison also the, by then useless, perambulator undercarriage wheels. This would, of course, necessitate a re-alignment between base board and body position, but Wally must be ever aware of the fluctuating conditions of real human flight and react accordingly. It only required then for them to nail a wooden orange box up front on the base board; this to contain his goggles, a large plastic carton of orange juice, an alarm clock, some food items, a modicum of personal needs, and Wally was ready. All that was needed now to bring the whole complex project to its ultimate fruition was a period of favourable prevailing weather. For this circumstance they waited with ever increasing impatience.

At last the agreed 'optimum weather' day arrived. They took the plane, now christened, 'The Yorkshire Canary' up to the top of the slag heap overlooking the cemetery. Word had got out, and, as Joe wound and trigger loaded the propeller, a small group of rubber-necking locals took up station a short distance away. Wally climbed aboard, and strapped himself in. He then turned to Joe for some final instructions. Joe, his voice tight with emotion, spoke softly.

"Pillage favourable thermals, glide and soar as much as possible. Use your alarm clock wisely, for catnaps are all you can afford. Eat your snacks regularly, and as for toilet arrangements, needs must as the devil drives! I don't need to remind you Wally that if the first few wing strokes, or your aileron position are fluffed, then you won't be going very far." Joe, as he spoke, was pointing down to the cemetery 200 feet below their launch pad. Wally, now tense and tight lipped, nodded an unspoken farewell, and, with a look of gratitude in Joe's direction, reached forward for the trigger. A trigger which when activated, would unleash the pent up power of the wooden propeller.

The results were shocking in their immediacy! Wally was at one instant in Joe's company, the next, two hundred feet up and desperately fighting to control 'The Yorkshire Canary'. As it dipped momentarily towards the graveyard, he instinctively readjusted his ailerons and pushed outwards on the wishbone mechanism. He felt the immediate and responsive lift. He tried again, and there was a concerted cheer from the spectators below. The world's first real human flight, instead of ending in the cemetery, as he and Joe had secretly feared; was now soaring confidently into Aviation's history books. Mankind would from now on remember that 28th of November when Barnsley, in world annals, became famous for even more than the proverbial fifteen minutes.

Joe, gazing up at a Wally now swooping exuberantly as he displayed his new found power; was harbouring very mixed emotions. Wally soared, flew, banked, dived and circled in a seemingly cavalier, but totally controlled fashion. Then, with a figure of eight manoeuvre and a waggle of his wings he turned eastwards into the far distance, emitting a faint, strangled cry which sounded remarkably like 'adios!' Joe watched for a long time and at last turned to go home, his face wet with unaccustomed tears. But whether his tears were tears of sorrow, or of pride and joy, not even the most up to date mass spectrometer could have possibly analysed.

The months passed, Winter into Spring, and the absent Wally's life disappeared, bit by bit, in front of Joe's worried eyes. One Monday morning there was an eager new face digging up Wally's long cherished allotment. The council, Joe heard, had repossessed Wally's flat; giving the total contents of same to the Sally Army. Ugly rumour gathered and persisted that Wally had really last been seen getting onto a Manchester train with his neighbour's wife. An otherwise blameless lady who had coincidentally opted for the acherontic shades round about that point in time. No man indeed was a hero in his own land, not even the unfortunate Wally.

Now harbouring deep despair, Joe's visits to John Barleycorn became more regular. And it was while he was recounting, for the umpteenth time, Wally's probable tragedy; that a young eavesdropper in the 'Fox and Widget' piped up.

"Why don't you surf the information highway mate? You know, the internet! That's where all the world's information thing is happening now. If your friend Wally has left any traces of his unusual existence on Terra Firma, you can bet that the web's where they'll show up."

Seeing Joe's look of abject puzzlement, he paused and groaned inwardly.

"You know mate, we're talking here about the 21st Century communication system. I'm an expert on it! Between jobs at the moment of course! Look, why don't you bring me up some relevant information, and we'll see if we can surf the highway for you. What say tomorrow evening, 26 Acorn Road, name's Pete by the way, what's yours? And don't say a flippen' pint of Guinness!"

As arranged, Joe duly turned up at Pete's house, there to gaze with growing amazement upon the young computer engineer's plethora of wires, computers, screens, printouts and winking displays. So this was the technology which had buried forever his own dated knowledge of world communication? Pete input the date of Wally's departure as the starting point for the internet search. He then began to download all the relevant information contained in the 'wacky World' megabyte. The eureka factor had almost passed off the display screen before Joe's inexperienced eye finally took it in. There, right in front of him, were the pulsating words . . .

Nov 29th London. 08. 30 hours:
>   Last night a wooden propeller hurtled down from the sky onto
>   static traffic. Junction 3. M25 Motorway – Police in a spin –
>   Stanstead, Gatwick and Heathrow deny all knowledge.

Eureka! they had isolated their first clue. Wally must have jettisoned the prop as planned when he'd attained confidence. Now, what else could this fantastic new technology unveil about the unfortunate Wally? Joe readied a writing pad, and, pen poised, gazed eagerly at the pulsating screen once more.

When, three hours later, he eventually said his grateful goodbye to Pete, Joe carried with him the whole story, well, almost the whole story, of Wally and the first ever man powered flight. In the follow-on from the M25 Motorway clue; the complete read-out now revealed.

Nov 29th. 07.15 hrs. Gibraltar:
>   Coupled perambulator wheels plummet down onto roof of

106

Europa Sporting Club. Authorities convinced that someone is off their trolley . . .

Nov 30th. 16.00 hrs. Cairo:
Airways pilot reports sighting of large yellow bird over desert verified by camel train bound for Hurghada . . . Egyptian doctors demand pay rise.

Dec 2nd. 11.00 hrs. New Delhi:
Plummeting alarm clock startles sacred cow in Sujan Singh Park. Investigators are carefully piecing together its every movement . . .

Dec 4th. 16.17 hrs. Perth, W Australia:
Large parcel of human excrement wrapped in English newspaper *Barnsley Bugle*, dated Nov 28th, lands in Hay Street. Puzzled officials are going through the motions . . .

Then came, what to Joe was not only the last, but potentially the most ominous read-out of them all. His vision blurred as he read again the stark, chilling message.

Dec 11th. 17.24 hrs. Belo Horizonte, Brazil:
A strange yellow kite was seen to circle before seemingly impacting into clearing in Matto Grosso; this some 200km due north of report point. Investigators working on theory that power unit may have run out of juice . . .

As he re-read the copied download, Joe's eyes began to glisten once more. The landing method had always been going to create a problem. And Wally? If he had survived the final impact, he just might still be alive – still out there in that South American wilderness. A feeling of abject helplessness racked for a moment his sorrowing frame. Wally, the first man to accomplish the impossible! The first man to overcome the seeming impossibility of virtual human flight; and how! Only for it all to end silently in this anti climax. No! Joe swore to himself, it could not be! Poor

Wally deserved better than this, he deserved the fame, the universal applause. And all he seemed to be getting from an ungrateful world was an anonymous dive into the oblivious arms of a dark and hostile Brazilian Jungle.

The more he pondered the situation, the more agitated Joe was to become; it was all so bloody unfair! But what could he himself do to solve the problem? If only poor Wally, assuming he was still alive, could be rescued? Given at least a fighting chance to savour his deserved moment of world acclamation. But how? How? Joe's look of deep and utter despair was suddenly replaced by a smile of almost ethereal joy. He would have to have some help of course, maybe Pete? Still pondering, he put on his jacket, left his council flat, and made his way down to the Kennedy Street Timber Warehouse. After more than an hour's careful examination he finally bought a sturdy plank of approximately three metres in length. That was the first objective attained, now for the undercarriage. He knew just exactly where a suitable pair of buggy wheels could be obtained, and that merely for the asking. His face now much more relaxed, and a jaunty spring in his step, he shouldered his plank, and began to sing quietly to himself, "Yellow Bird, high up in Banana Tree . . ."

15
Dust

Down on the ash-covered pitch it was a ding-dong battle between the Gasworks Select and a team from the Power Station. Dust spurted up from the tackles, which were sometimes a little too fierce and over enthusiastic. The shrill rallying cries of the opposing supporters dotted around the perimeter of the football pitch resounded hollowly from the time-blackened brickwork of the nearby retort-house.

Within the huge, now disused old building, the cries from the football match echoed eerily. Even drowning the angry cries of those pigeons disturbed by Jimmy as he advanced nimbly along the inner roof girders. Swiftly, methodically, he traversed the hazardous maze of girder-work, his probing blue eyes raking every nook and ledge for more pigeons' eggs. The birds, as they reluctantly retreated before his relentless advance, blew clouds of dust from the girder tops with every beat of their panicky wings.

Sure-footed in his tattered baseball boots, Jimmy stopped occasionally, one arm tightly clutching the nearest support beam, and unthinkingly raped another hurriedly deserted roost. Some eggs, still warm, he considered to be too small. These he dropped from his grubby fingers in disgust. The other boys at the school would only pay him for the really big ones.

The rejects, as they hit the rusting bogie rails nearly a hundred feet below, burst like miniature bombs, each one exploding and sending its shattered contents high into the air. Sometimes a stray sunbeam, as it poked a bright finger through the latticed brickwork, would catch the showering egg fluid and, for a brief moment, would turn the droplets into what seemed to wee Jimmy like some sort of daylight fireworks – the penny sparkler kind.

He paused to rest and count his spoils. Fourteen beauties! Each one worth three pence a time easy. Maybe even four pence. Six more good big ones and he would chuck it at that. Down on the football pitch someone had scored a goal. The applause, as it reached a new crescendo, distracted his thoughts for a moment.

"Football! A stupid game that, only fit for people who were afraid to go egg hunting."

Jimmy started forward again, but this time his advance was blocked by one of the old retort feed boxes. With all those eggs in his lumber jacket pocket now, he would have to be extra careful. The precious load was making it more and more difficult to balance on the dust-laden girders.

Already his denims and his good red pullover, especially knitted for Christmas by Auntie Sadie who had looked after him since Ma died, were completely covered in grey powdery dust. His hair and face, too, had become granite grey in the cloying, dust-laden atmosphere. A smile creased Jimmy's caked lips. All the other boys were afraid of the high girders, but they were eager enough to pay him for the big eggs. Pete Adams had tried to climb up with him once though – what a laugh that had turned out to be. Jimmy smiled again, remembering how he had had to rescue his tear-faced pal patiently coaxing and guiding his trembling legs to safety from a measly height of only about forty feet.

As he surmounted the retort box hazard, another cheer from the football field flooded the comparative silence.

Another goal for someone. Jimmy smiled the cynical smile of a ten-year-old nearing eleven. Then he jumped out boldly on to another girder and started to probe another dark, inviting ledge.

It was getting warmer inside the old retort-house now. The smell of tar was becoming much stronger as warm fingers of sunlight caressed the long-dead seal pots, stirring them momentarily to new life. To Jimmy it was a pleasant, comforting smell. After rejecting the contents of three nests in a row, he found another acceptable specimen. It was lodged under a retort

110

box marked twenty-three by a long gone operator. That made nineteen now. Only one more to go. But what would Auntie Sadie say when she saw his pullover? He shuddered the thought away.

He moved even more carefully now, the dust having become an impenetrable blanket beneath his probing feet. Jimmy balanced himself and stepped out confidently towards the next girder. There, he had made it all right! But why was he hurtling through the seemingly solid girder? He grabbed at the girder with his hands as he passed — no need for panic; this had happened before. But his searching fingers found only dust and he was falling — falling. His terrified scream was drowned out by a triumphant roar from the spectators as the ball found the net once more. The pigeons sought their ravaged roosts. Dust settled — and the treacherous girder, a mere shadow cast on the dust cloud by a sun-kissed vertical stay, gradually disappeared.

On the ground Jimmy lay very still, his lips a strange purple colour under the dust mask. His blue eyes open and questing, a sort of half-smile seeming to play on those strange tinted lips. The egg fluid seeping from his pockets was coursing slowly towards the fluid which oozed from his shattered skull. As they met, the fluids merged in embryonic affinity; a stray sunbeam framing the scene and casting a warm seal of approval on the strange union.

Out on the football pitch the final whistle blew. The crowd gave a last hoarse cheer and began to drift away. Another game was over, the Gasworks had finally won. But wee Jimmy, the school egg collecting champion, hadn't really been in the least bit interested in football.

When Fred, the security man, found him that evening, the sun's rays had gone from the scene. But Jimmy's eyes, as they gazed on out past the char valves and the grimy gas engine which had once driven them, were now strangely gentle. Onwards, outwards, he gazed. Far beyond all the outposts of the rational concept. On what Elysian field that gaze finally came to focus, God alone knew. But wee Jimmy must have spotted a friend out there, for he was still smiling. Fred directed his torch beam high up into the girders. The resultant agitation in the shadowy heights caused a trickle of dust to descend into his upturned eyes. He blinked, and knew from long experience that his eyes would soon water. It was the fourth, or maybe the fifth time this year that the pigeons had fluttered, and won.

16

A Conflict of Outcomes

Early August '96, Weisenthal's group eventually tracked Dorfmann down to a shack in the Santos Dumont suburb of Rio. He was a solitary old man now, so old indeed that they had to carefully double check his identity. Satisfied at last, the basic details were then faxed to Mossad in Tel Aviv. That organisation, again displaying an efficiency previously evidenced at The King David Hotel incident, The Eichmann snatch and the Vanunu affair, swung swiftly into action. This with a calculated professionalism which would have left the world, had it ever known about it, suitably astounded.

A week later, on the Thursday afternoon, as Dorfmann was shambling homeward from the International Friendship Club on the Rua Da Matriz; three casually clad but very efficient agents mobbed him. Before he could even think about mustering up a protest, they had unceremoniously bundled his faltering old frame into a hovering black limo. Sure, a few passing rubbernecks momentarily checked their stride. But while they were coming to terms with yet another South American 'Desaparado'; the limo had accelerated smoothly down the Rua Bolivar with Hans Dorfmann's feebly protesting form now shrouded in a voluminous dark blue beach towel.

Less than ten minutes later, he found himself being hustled towards the rear door of the safe house on Avenida Niemeyer. So far it had all worked out beautifully. But then again, Mossad Agents had had plenty of practice in such operations. Their record

113

stretching back almost to the Holocaust itself.

The towel eventually removed, Hans blinked confusedly, focused his rheumy blue eyes, then surveyed the four righteous males who were ritually busying themselves round his chair. He had by this time guessed what was to follow, but he felt little fear, only a surge of too long pent up relief. True, at this critical moment he could have done with the comfort of his angina pills, but what the hell! Where was a man going anyway at the age of 78?

The smallest one, whom the others addressed as Moshe, sat at the rear of the room, pen poised to take notes. In front of Hans stood the suave interrogator whom the others referred to as Beni; and by his side, cradling a machine pistol, sat the one they called Simon. While slowly shuffling around between the room and an adjoining kitchen was the fourth member of the squad; an elderly grey haired dog's-body, who's name he was destined never to discover.

Beni spoke first, betraying a decidedly mid-Atlantic accent. "Well Mr Dorfmann, so we finally get to meet! Not since you disappeared down The Odessa Trail in Italy in '45 have we managed to flush you out. And to be honest, we wouldn't even be looking for you now. Except that you've surfaced in the world press as some sort of latter day revisionist historian. We knew you back then as a mere nonentity; a non event little SS Corporal. What's with this new role you've adopted as expert on Zionist affairs?"

Hans, tongue washing his dry lips, answered in a hoarse, crackling voice. "I guess I got sick of being an uneducated Aryan lout, no mileage in that. After mastering in modern history at Sao Paulo a long while back, I was driven eventually to do something with my new found knowledge of world affairs. This even though the prevailing tide was against me. The silencing of Palestinian history, and its replacement by the crude invention of ancient exodus Israelis being the bedrock of modern Zionism triggered my latent sense of fair play. I found out that the Exodus, with or without its eagle's wings, washed up in the then watering holes along the Southern Med, and nowhere near present day Israel. A

114

transcript of a lecture given by a Professor Keith Whitelam of Scotland's Stirling University verified my findings. He gave his lecture on June 12th '96 at London's School of Oriental & African Studies. It was a masterpiece of honest endeavour and lucidity, delivered by a learned man with no particular racial or even political axe to grind. Surely Mossad had an observer there? Or are you lads strictly limited to Orthodox Jewish views of history?"

Ignoring the taunting tone inherent in the questions, Beni referred once more to the sizeable sheaf of newspaper cuttings in his hand. "Then there's your second theory, which argues that Lord Rothschild actually bought from a beleaguered Britain in 1917 the famous Balfour Declaration; a paper which would allow a harassed Jewish Diaspora to enter Palestine legally? This decision, you argue, torpedoed the hopes of Lawrence of Arabia; who seemingly had been promising various assorted Arabs their desert lands back in return for helping Great Britain to eject the recalcitrant Turks from the sands of Palestine. You seem to be operating from fairy-tale land now Hans, I bet Lawrence finished up even more disappointed than his Arab friends. A bit funny wasn't he? That is, before he was literally rubbed out of the annals of history by a mysterious car accident."

"A black car, just like yours! But I guess maybe that was just coincidence. More probably Lawrence was at last proving a mite obdurate, and the British arranged his early demise themselves. The only people who say there's no future in history are those who've benefited from its passing. However, I digress; to be blunt about it, nowhere in the Balfour Declaration are Zionists given the green light to use Arab citizens as second class expendables."

Once more ignoring the barbed statement, Beni asked with saccharin sweetness. "And what exactly did we, the Jews, pay for the Balfour Declaration in 1917, Mr Dorfmann?"

"Well, if I can quote Mr Fisher, a member of the British cabinet who composed the declaration. His 1935 book, *A History of Europe*, tells us. 'By proclaiming its intention to establish in Palestine a national home for the Jews, Great Britain rallied to the Allied cause, at a time when money was urgently needed, the

115

powerful and cosmopolitan community, which, not from New York alone, controls the loan markets of the world.' So, if I may be allowed to analyse. The pressurised Jewish Diaspora had been seeking for a decade or more a foothold in Palestine. In 1917, after three years of attritious war with Germany, Britain was broke, with no early victory in sight. Lawrence had just managed to liberate Palestine. The Jews had money, they wanted a legal entry into Palestine. The deal, brokered in the Balfour Declaration, deliberately negated Lawrence's earlier promise to the Arabs. 'So what!' you might say, but when Fisher's book hit the markets in '35, it rightly or wrongly portrayed German Jews as a cross between fifth columnists, and Germany's enemy within. It has to be accepted that Jewish partisan financial involvement in World War One, when coupled to Adolf Hitler's rise to power in Germany, could result in only one inevitable genocidal consequence. I refer of course to that tragic final solution, the subsequent Holocaust, with its crystal night, its horrendous gas oven executions and its zyklon B exterminations. It was a terrible price your race had to pay gentlemen for the hasty and inopportune purchase of an illegitimate patch of now heavily barb-wired middle eastern desert. Or don't you think so?"

"What we think is our business Hans, it's what you and the rest of the world thinks that occupies Mossad."

Beni, pausing after his out of character outburst, then turned to Simon, whose machine pistol was very much in evidence.

"How do you read this one Simon?"

The latter, his face still set in menace mode snarled, "Where does he get this shit from Beni? We spend too much time listening to these Nazi apologists. I suggest we just go ahead and rub him . . ."

"Now, now Simon, the first rule is we must try to understand the anti-Semite sector of Gentile society. We must attempt to draw the sting, all this for our future reference of course. Still taking those notes for posterity moshe?"

As the scribe grunted a hasty affirmative, Beni turned his expressionless gaze once more towards Hans. "Hans, Hans why do you insist in persecuting the Jews? Haven't we suffered

116

enough from such rabid anti-Semitic negative career move diatribes? Tell me now, just where are you coming from?"

"Well, since you asked, I don't happen to be anti-Semitic thank you. I just happen to believe that Jews, especially the arrogant self righteous element, have no God given right to regard themselves as being somehow above objective criticism, no matter from which source. That can't be right, no person or race is that perfect. For fifty odd years now the west's collective conscience has been bombarded by your cynical Holocaust industry. Relentless media films and now museums proclaim your great historical tragedy. But let me enlighten you! Your glib six million Holocaust figure takes no account whatever that a half million victims were non-Jewish gypsies, about the same number were Germany's mentally unbalanced, and at least a further half million were Aryan anti-Nazi dissidents. Add to that the large number of Jews who died, arguably naturally, from Typhus and other illnesses in the camps, and your six million Jews claim would be, by any fair statistical system, ripe for a modicum of downsizing. And don't forget that concentration camps happen to be a British Boer war invention. Some died there also I believe! Can you explain why the Russians, who lost nearly twelve million citizens in the Second World War, have managed to resist making an industry out of such a tragic historical fact?"

"Maybe they don't care so much about their citizens Hans; Jews are not so ordinary, I don't say that we're really a chosen race, but you won't find many of us in the sweat industries, except maybe those of us who run them of course, that's different! You must surely have recognised our obvious business and intellectual gifts by now Hans?"

"Of course I do Beni. For the cost of a meal and a tube of toothpaste the youth of the world are making your many kibbutz bloom. All this as the cream of today's Jewish Diaspora is becoming famous for its more than nodding acquaintance with the God Mammon. Looking objectively over the Middle East, I wouldn't say that you are all bully boys in the best Nazi mould. But it would take a lot of fast talking to explain away Sabra, Chatila and Qana. Sure, you've lost some fine citizens in return,

117

mostly to disaffected Arabs. But to my way of thinking, the casualties you have sustained in your 'occupied' territories don't even enter the equation. And, what with the arbitrary imposition of new settlements, coupled to the demolition of dissident Arab homes, Israel today could be likened to the proverbial whited sepulchre. Lapped around its perimeter by arrogantly ignored United Nations resolutions, 242, 338, and 425. With Uncle Sam hovering around as your guarantor. Congratulations gentlemen on your unlimited supply of atomic weapons! Vanunu exposed that one, at a price, poor Mr Vanunu! But woe betide any of your neighbour countries who would dare to seek parity. If you're not knocking out the occasional Iraqi power station, or the equally inconvenient Iranian one, you're eliminating potential gnats like Mr Bull, 'The engineer', or the occasional indiscreet Mullah. Uncle Sam intervenes now and then to sort out the more serious spats. Such, for instance, as the fairly recent Gulf War. Yes indeed, Israel has at last become a mighty nation. One bent on stopping, by whatever means, her first military defeat. And manufacturing in the process a steady output of endemic pan anti-Semitism. Not for you the structures imposed by the ten commandments and all that 'Love thy neighbour' guff. That was discarded when you chose Barabbas. And getting back for a moment to the mundane level. Why do you Israeli's implacably watch as fuel prices soar around the world? Can't you make the quantum leap and accept some responsibility?"

As the now very hoarse Hans Dorfmann paused for breath, Simon, his voice tight with ill contained menace, interrupted the silence.

"Do we really have to listen to any more of this crap Beni? Let's at least ship him home to Tel-Aviv – you know! The public show trial treatment! He may not have directly been guilty of any crime – you can't go to gaol for what you're thinking. But as you've said yourself often enough, he's a still living symbol of Nazism and the Holocaust, and there are now very few left. His physical presence at a public show trial would help to perpetuate the memory. We owe it to the next generation for God's sake! We've snared the sort of guy whom you find anywhere in the

118

world, daubing defamation's onto Jewish synagogues or around our graveyards. Hans here sees the Munich Massacre or the Achille Lauro incident as being some sort of just retribution for Zionism's past actions. Isn't that so Hans?"

Dorfmann pondered the heated question for a moment then answered.

"Every action Simon, has to have an equal and opposite reaction. That is an irrefutable scientific fact. And anti-Semitism is a reactive disease. The Balfour Declaration negotiators and your later anti-Arab decisions in Knesset show us for sure that what the Zionist government sows, the unprotected Jewish Diaspora will usually reap. And you will undoubtedly find parallels to this theory hovering around every so called terrorist situation you care to name. The holocaust's tragic happening gives you, as a race, no automatic right to immunity from criticism for your subsequent actions. World respect can only be gained by deeds, not bought by force or deception. OK you probably don't agree with what I say, but as so called democrats you should be recognising my right to say it. Otherwise, we're just replacing Hitler's form of fascism with Israel's. To me at least, my proofs are irrefutable, if there are flaws, I most assuredly apologise."

It was then that the nameless man spoke.

"Let's keep our resolve. As we listen to this man, our buses are being blown up, our people ambushed and killed. At the reality level, mortgages in Jaffa are high, and the financial rewards from our present mission are inextricably linked to its successful conclusion."

Beni, showing some signs of agitation, snapped back at his colleagues. "Slow down men! Eichmann and Vanunu were in some ways counter productive. We've caught a lobster here, this guy really believes, his mind is fizzing. And, at a public trial, given the wrong defence lawyer and views that are capable of misinterpretation he too might upset our game plan. Hans is a very dangerous witness. We must get rid of . . ."

Before he could finish his sentence, Simon butted in: "I have no problem whatever with that suggestion Beni, and I have here

119

the little bit of hardware that can accomplish the task. Only say the word . . ." As Simon affectionately patted his machine pistol, Hans had a sudden premonition that the whole goddam exercise was now taking on a new and much more sinister turn of events. Where did the interrogation end and the retribution begin? If he were to be eventually freed, would he remember their identities? He scanned their faces individually and with some care for a long moment. Even knowing their forenames was nothing more than an empty exercise. For weren't these people chameleon-like in their ability to tactically name change should the situation call for it? Many an Anglo Saxon clan had woken up one morning to discover that they now had a semite branch. So much indeed for that proud Jewish ancestry! He was just about to formulate a sarcastic barb about Simon's embracing the SS philosophy, when suddenly the pain hit him, just as Doctor Fernandez had warned. The spasms tortured his left arm first, then there was that awful crushing restriction in his chest. When a second wave of pain followed, he realised instinctively that this latest heart attack was not only for real, but that it was undoubtedly going to prove terminal.

Early next morning, well before the first sun worshippers were heading for their daily wrestle with skin cancer; the departing Mid-East airliner spotted the body sprawled on the beach, and deeming it to be its moral duty, alerted the police.

There was a single bullet hole drilled through Hans' heart, but no blood had seeped from the wound. In one of his capacious tunic pockets they found eight expertly wrapped shots of heroin, and in another the police unearthed twelve thousand cruiseros, all in crisp, newly circulated notes, their serial numbers running in sequence.

In the *Saturday Herald*, on page five, and under the punning title, 'Hans across the sea', Raul, their crime reporter, waxed lyrical. As the article unfolded, he speculated intelligently about Hans' probable involvement in a long running feud amongst the local drug barons, an evil trade that had probably been, for some years now, financing an opulent lifestyle for the old German. Before, that was, the inevitable tentacles of retribution had caught up with the vile pusher on a cold, deserted, early morning beach. Ignoring the mundane facts had signally failed to kill a good story.

Three evenings later, down in the Rio City Morgue, just as the sun was setting behind the huge statue of Christ the Redeemer atop the Corcovado mountain, they began to prepare Hans for his state managed burial. And, not even when they at last got round to lowering the coffin lid, did that fixed, enigmatic smile depart from his lined old face.

f

17

The Con Game

Arthur absent-mindedly masticated the last piece of toast, drained his mug, and then lowered the *Daily Record*. A sullen grey sky was peering in through the misted window. He muttered a cynical, "Hail scowling morn!" and rose reluctantly from the cosy kitchen table.

As he passed the front door, on the way to his room, the letter-box disgorged its contents, closing again with a vicious snap. Arthur stooped and scanned the imposingly franked letter; it was for him. His heart started to thump with excitement, he took the letter, made for his room, and hurriedly closed the door. It took but a moment to find the broken ebony paper-knife he'd bought for twenty pence at The Barrows. It tore raggedly into the envelope, he removed the letter and focussed hopefully onto the contents:

'Dear Sir,
    With regard to your recent application for employment in this household, we regret to inform you that on this occasion . . .'

"Damnation!"

Oh well, so that was that. He wasn't going to be butler at Windsor Castle after all. To be fair to the Duke though, the fact that he, Arthur, had never buttled before had no doubt swayed the decision more than a little. But anyway, he reflected sagely, 'Blessed are they who go through life expecting nothing, for they assuredly shall not end up disappointed.' But enough of this dallying in that Lotus-land called, 'might have been'. He tore the letter of rejection into pieces and dropped them into the waste bin. Something was sure to turn up. Maybe even tomorrow, it was all a simple matter of perseverance.

After all, hadn't he hit the bar a few times. Like last November for instance. He'd almost been voted onto the Board of the new Health Authority Trust. Then, at the final hurdle, they inadvertently discovered that he was already in their employ – as a hospital porter.

So near, and yet so far. Arthur's ears still tingled every time he recalled the Trust Chairman's frosty comments. The little fat geezer, his hands quivering agitatedly behind his back, had slowly paced the musty, oak panelled conference room. How had his speech ended? Ah yes: " . . . and as much as we all admire a hospital porter with, er, drive; ladies and gentlemen. I really don't think that our weekly paid work people should be encouraged to sit in at board meetings. Even democracy has its limits . . ."

Arthur had immediately given up the job. After all, there was a principle involved. But he'd noticed, with not a little bitterness, that his departure had not created many waves.

But new doors were forever opening, like the short period he'd recently spent as a film director with NGM. In his letter of application he'd intimated that in the Glasgow area he'd no mean reputation as a play actor. It hadn't been all that big a lie really, more a sort of sparing with the actuality. For his friends had been calling him a play actor for more years than he'd honestly cared to recall.

Sure, Arthur had got the position all right. But they'd caught up with him during a rush demo take. So who the hell knew everything about rebated camera angle anyway? And as for the male lead, surely a victim of dramatic fever? Arthur had often witnessed a better performance turned in by a thirsty hobo outside The Citizens on a Friday night. That job too was now well behind him. After the humiliating negative exposure, he had exited from the studios stage left, bearing a month's salary and a very temporary grudge.

Despite the greyness of the sky, the air wafting in through his window now seemed a little warmer. He picked up the morning paper once more, squared his shoulders, and began to study the 'Crown Posts Abroad' section. The financial inducements brought a gleam to his watery blue eyes.

'Coconut Inspector on Christmas Island'. What more could one want? Plenty of decision making of course, but it only required a modicum of common sense to differentiate a good coconut from a bad one, definitely worth a bash. Ah! There was another position worth gambling a stamp on. 'Crown Agent for Mauritius – must possess a good knowledge of figures.' A veritable piece of cake, for who knew more about figures, one way or another, than he did? Hadn't he been studying them with more than a little pleasure for years now? And anyway. All that Crown Agents did was collect royalties from the sugar or banana wallahs, thank them very much, and then wield their official rubber stamps with the gay abandon commonly displayed by servants of Her Majesty's realm. All in all, it was now proving to be a fruitful morning after all. He reached for his pen, positioned the writing pad and began:

'Dear Sirs,
    In reply to your recent advertisement in . . .'

Arthur had just completed his fourth application of the morning, when old Ma McGregor, his long suffering landlady, made her appearance.

"This just arrived in the second post, Arthur. Who do you know in Moscow anyway?" Her voice oozed suspicion.

"Oh, from Moscow, is it? That'll be the reply to the second Press Attaché's position I applied for last month!"

"What exactly do you know about that kind of work, you haven't been a Press At . . . whatever it was – before, have you?"

"Of course I haven't been a Press Attaché before, Ma, but, don't you see, it's all a matter of common sense. I read the papers every day, don't I? And that's what this job's all about, after all."

"I suppose you know what you're doing!" Ma sounded as

though she didn't. "But news is printed in Russian out that way Arthur, a wee point worthy of your consideration. And it'll take a wee bit more than mere common sense to translate it!"

Before Arthur could formulate a suitable reply, she threw him a speculative sidelong glance, and left the room. News printed in Russian! The old dear had made a valid point there. Arthur, half hoping he wouldn't get the position after all, tore the crested envelope open with nervous fingers. Come to think about it, Moscow could be cold at any time of year, so why was he risking pneumonia just to satisfy some wild personal ambition? Andy Higgins, the clerk down at the Social Security, was forever advising him to content himself at home. Arthur never argued with Andy, for the clerk meant well, and was too nice a guy to quarrel with. But no Social Security advisor had the moral right to stop Arthur reaching for the stars if he chose to do so.

He threw the envelope into the bucket, and turned his attention to the contents. It began with the usual Civil Service Blali-Blah, and then continued:

' . . .We are therefore prepared to offer you the position, and, subject to our conditions being acceptable to you, we would be grateful if you would take time to advise us as to the date at which you could commence work at our Moscow Embassy.'

Arthur's eyes gleamed in triumph. Eureka! But wait a minute – his eyes narrowed perceptibly, as though some problem had reared its ugly head. Yes, there was undoubtedly a problem. Ma McGregor had set the ball of doubt rolling with her shrewd observation that Arthur didn't understand Russian. And here they were, offering the position regardless. There had to be a catch in it somewhere. There just had to be. Arthur slowly re-read the letter, mouthing every word. Still no catch. Whichever way he studied it, it seemed a genuine offer. But Moscow in winter? It would be even worse than Ma McGregor's digs. Now if it had been Madrid or Athens or even Casablanca, he'd have walked there backwards as the saying went. But Moscow? Whatever had possessed him to write such a job application. It stood to reason that the really qualified people would be shunning the place because of the conditions – the cold and stuff. Yes, that was it – they were going to have him for a mug. But he was too long in the tooth to fall for that one. His lips now tightening with new found resolve, Arthur reached for the pen he'd won for the star letter in, *The Weekly News*, and began to write, slowly and deliberately.

'Sirs,
    With regard to your recent offer of employment as Second Press Attaché in Moscow, I'm sorry that I must decline your very generous offer, this due to a recently diagnosed medical condition. I nevertheless thank you for your interest in my application, and wish you every success in your search for a more suitable applicant.
    Yours etc.'

There, that would put them off. A clever touch, the medical bit. With a sigh of satisfaction he reached for another envelope, addressed it, and enclosed the letter. Arthur then relaxed, stretched luxuriantly, and began to speculate as to whether it would be sausage and mash or fish for lunch.

After lunch – it had proved to be sausage and mash after all – he shaved, dressed leisurely, and left the house. Once out in the street, the grey sky had fled, and the sun was now splitting the tenements. Along the streets the girls were proudly strutting incipient fecundity. Their fashions were numerous, their designs unchanging. Arthur wandered listlessly down to the Social Security office, and queued up resignedly behind an old unemployable. His friendly greeting was met with a rye smile. Oh well, pay day again, and not before time either. One seemed to spend so much money, time and energy on this job hunting lark.

When he finally reached the desk, Andy looked up, saw him, and gave him a friendly, "Hi, Arthur, I see you've brought the sunshine with you!"

"Sure have, Andy."

"Here's your delayed cheque Arthur, sorry about that. Had any luck with your job search since we last saw you?"

"No, nothing yet, Andy. Only an Assistant Press Attaché's job in Moscow. I think I mentioned it to you a while back, but I turned it down. The temperature over that way kinda swayed the issue for me. Anything doing at this end?"

"Well, we've had no word about that boilerman's job down at the Tannery yet, Arthur. You're first in line of course. There's another vacancy here, just came in, which you might fancy though."

Andy leafed through his indexed file, withdrew a card, and checked it on his monitor screen.

"Advertising Assistant, must be young, imaginative and have integrity, how does that sound to you, Arthur?"

"Advertising? Thanks, but no thanks, Andy. Those people tend to play around too much with life's certitudes."

"Fair enough, Arthur, I'll probably see you next week. Maybe something will have turned up by then."

Arthur thanked Andy, pocketed his cheque, and turned away. Behind a neighbouring desk a young Asian interview clerk was asking a grizzled Irish labourer if he'd ever considered the idea of moving to Australia for work. Arthur shut his ears to the invective studded reply, and wandered out into the welcome sunshine.

The warmth of the day re-kindled a surge of determination and resolve within his sparse frame. Despite the temporary career setbacks, it was still good to be alive. "Who knows," he reflected with growing optimism, "Maybe next month I'll be heading out to Mauritius, or even Christmas Island. That'll give them something to talk about down at Paddy's Market."

A pillar box loomed into view, he fed his letters into its hungry red slit of a mouth with a confident flourish. He didn't really feel all that hopeful, but remembering the Moscow result. Hell! In this world you had to at least look the part. A few minutes later, as he was sauntering past Harry's Grocer Shop; Jean, the young assistant came out, and threw him a smile that was like a lasso. He reluctantly ducked the warm invitation, and she, sensing this from his half hearted return smile, immediately froze the emotion. Poor kid! But he was being hurtful for her own good really. He fancied her, and she knew it. If only he could try a

127

little . . . But what was the use? Girls, like Jean, had obviously never ever read *Love On The Dole*.

On his way to the library, Arthur's route took him past Guido's Café. From the juke-box, situated behind the potato crisp cartons, a haunting melody started up and drifted out toward his sensitive ears. Then, from a recklessly opened tenement window, a crying baby took up the chorus. Arthur, sensing his cue, began, slightly off key, to whistle the refrain. As the tune, now recognisable as being, *I'm Forever Blowing Bubbles*, rent the now tepid air, two sparrows rose from a gutter banquet in panic flight. Spring, the uninvited, had wheedled its way, yet again, into the reluctant heart of Glasgow.

18

The Things of the State

Almost from the day he had been admitted, old Joe Gillan had hated the cloying hospital smells; added to that, everything in the damned ward was so clinically clean and unlived in. Not at all like his old abode in Baltic Street, in the living-room of which the smoking stove was forever dulling the brass terrier on his cluttered mantelpiece. The roof of his flat leaked too of course, but happily only if the rain was being driven up from the direction of the Clyde.

How long had he been kicking his heels in this hospital now? Six, nearly seven weeks. All the time tests and more bloody tests; then there were the pills, tons of the ruddy things, ranging from vitamins and dietary ones through to laxatives and aspirin; man alive! If someone shook him now, he'd probably rattle!

Around him scurried nurses worried more about bed closures, their jobs, their mortgages or their grading than they did about their patients' welfare. As a friendly caring environment this particular hospital had proved to be the pits. It was of little use trying to view the real world from the hospital window either. Joe had tried that once or twice. But the invariable scene which had met his rheumy eyes had proved to be serried ranks of grotty tombstones.

"Some ruddy view; that's where the surgeon's hide their bleedin' mistakes out there Joe."

Thus had old Alf in the next bed summed up their surrounds.

Joe had had to smile at that one, but there wasn't much else to smile about. Hadn't Evans, the top Consultant even stopped them from having an occasional flutter on the nags with the local Turf Accountant? Something about it being a too exciting pastime for them at their age. Where Joe hailed from, there was a definite name for the Doctor Evans' of this world.

Then, to crown it all, just a week ago, old Alf had up and died on him. One minute his usual loveable old moaning self, the next, dead, just like that! Joe sorely missed him, even though he'd been a bloody Rangers supporter. Well, there was the odd good one, aye, maybe just one or two. And anyway, at times of shared adversity, the football rivalry thing tended to assume due proportion and pale into comparative insignificance.

Old Alf's bed had now been filled by a broken down stray from the posh end of the city. He was a private patient of Evans', an old ex-Army Colonel who proved to be on a very different wave length from Joe and made little or no attempt to narrow the social gap. Joe, marking him down as a pompous arsed old fogey, privately felt a little sorry for the guy, who, after all was said and done, had long ago lost the art of communicating with the real world.

As he now lay, eyes half closed, between the starched white sheets, Joe was watching with muted interest the everyday activity in the ward. Two orderlies were making up a bed, and fat, florid Doctor Evans, the one who according to Alf was making a bomb from his private patients, was on his routine rounds.

A bit of a mystery Evans; depending on who you spoke to, he was either a Doctor, a Consultant or a Hospital Trust Manager. But whatever you called him, he seemed to wield more than his share of authority. This fact becoming increasingly obvious to Joe as he quietly observed cleaners, orderlies and nurses upping their work rate at his mere presence.

Behind Evans was a thin, anaemic young surgeon called Mr Boyle, with the Ward Sister flapping along deferentially in the fat Consultant's rear. It reminded Joe of a poem he'd read once. How did it go again? 'Hail the conquering hero comes, leading his string of fawning bums . . .' Joe smiled to himself through half closed eyes, those poets knew a thing or two!

All the beds on the ward being full; like some bloated vulture, Evans waddled slowly from patient to patient. A pompous surveyal of the chart, a huddled conference with the tall, thin Doctor Boyle; a decision reached and imperious instruction to the anxiously hovering Sister, and then the slow procession would amble towards the next patient. It seemed to the observing Joe that Evans tended to reserve his occasional little encouraging smiles for his paying patients. But the dead Alf had clouded his critical judgement somewhat. And anyway, to Joe's way of thinking, the smiles had been kinda dearly bought. His own experience of having paid his weekly contributions into the system for forty years seemed to have counted for not a lot in the present health lottery.

When they eventually reached Joe's bed he had cunningly closed his eyes, composed his lined face and feigned slumber. Evans unhooked the chart at the bottom of the bed, studied it for a few brief moments, then remarked acidly.

"Symptoms of debilitation checked, patient responding. I see here that you recommend early heart surgery Boyle? Patient's last birthday, 74. Hardly worth the theatre time. Cost benefit analysis is not on your side. Fifty-fifty chance at best. And he'd occupy a bed for at least another two months of intensive recuperative treatment afterwards. Got to be all weighed in the balance you know! Social Worker's background report to hand Sister?"

"Yes Doctor Evans; he lives alone in the top flat of a crumbling old tenement. No known dependents or other relatives. Neighbours have testified to a cantankerous streak; some known debts . . . eats only porridge, usually straight from the cook pot. Has no foreseeable positive role in the furtherance of his society. A drain on scarce resources envisaged, this to the point of life termination. On the positive side, the psychologist has noted a spasmodic diminution of the will to live. Socially, subsistence level." As the sister ceased her recital of the social worker's report, Evans took up the commentary in a domineering fashion.

"As you can now see I'm sure Boyle, patching up the heart may suffice short term. But there are other fundamental and much more pressing considerations. After care problems are compounded by increasing pressure on available bed space. Here we have another old codger, past his sell by date. A man with no viable future, plugged into – and a very thirsty drain on – precious state resources. To be perfectly frank with you Boyle, Mr Gillan now adds up to being just another loser. An ideal candidate for terminal blue pill treatment. After all, in some circumstances it's now a perfectly legal conclusion to draw in our country."

In replying, Boyle's voice almost cracked; as he vainly attempted to control his pent up anger and emotion.

"You must give him a chance sir. Sure, when we thin the blood to repair the heart, his weeping piles may cause him to bleed to death. But he deserves his chance surely? Remember the Hippocratic Oath! We're here to save lives, not to callously terminate . . . to dispense designer death!"

"Now, now Mr Boyle, let's not start to wax emotional about this problem, try to be objective just this one time. As Manager of this hospital, I can only propound and support the survival of the fittest scenario. The reality is that this patient is in a tough old world and patently now really not well enough equipped to win, to adequately live outwith resources. He's a well spent force and that Mr Boyle is the grim reality. Sister! Bring the patient a cup of hot sweet tea, then wake him up. Oh, and bring one for me. One for you too Boyle?"

"No thank you sir!" As he spoke, Doctor Boyle's voice was trembling in an emotional disbelief which bordered almost on contempt.

Joe, listening with closed lids, began to shake uncontrollably for a brief moment. So this was what had happened to old Alf! And to God only knew how many before that. No longer positively viable, a drain on resources, now he was going to be next on the list. Some Doctors should now be made to take the Hypocritic Oath! After all, it was obviously a more truthful description of Evans' present 'Modus operandi'. Here he was, in hospital, once a haven of peace and tranquillity for the old and infirm, now having to accept an imposed death, voluntary suicide no less! Or to gather together his fading energy resources and fight the foul system. If that fat old bladder of lard Evans considered him to be . . ! Lost the will to live, had he? Not well enough equipped to survive, was he? After twelve years in the Commandos and forty years a steelworker? Evans or his system weren't going to be Joe's Waterloo. No sir! But he must remain cool, calm, think of something, make plans. He would ride this one, just like he'd done during that personal little triumph in Suez . . . or had it been Korea?

Joe now opened his eyes just wide enough to reconnoitre the scene. Doctor Boyle, head bowed, had his back to him. While Evans was just turning away after carefully laying a large, powdery blue pill on top of Joe's locker. Christ! If it had at least been a green pill! As he continued to watch, the Ward Sister trotted smartly down the ward with two cups of tea and laid them also on Joe's locker; one on either side of that menacing blue pill. She was just about to reach for the pill which would accelerate considerably Joe's demise, when Doctor Evans suddenly exclaimed. "Oh Sister! My general report sheet, I believe I've left it on your desk. I'll require it to fill in the exact time of Mr Gillan's . . . er . . . bed release. Could you fetch it for me?"

As the Sister sped off to obey this new request from her deity, the watching Joe had a sudden, desperate inspiration. Evans and Boyle were now chatting amiably to the ex-Colonel in the next bed. That exciting, now or never, moment had arrived. He slowly inched his hand out from under the bed clothes and up towards the offending pill. As his groping fingers at last found it, Joe then very surreptitiously picked it up and plopped it swiftly into the farthest away cup. There, no problem! But just in time.

He had no sooner withdrawn his hand and composed his lined old features once more into simulated slumber, when the Ward Sister came hurrying along the beds clutching the Hospital Manager's wayward general report sheet. Joe furtively watching the unfolding play of events, smiled inwardly. That was one report that should never have been mislaid. Evans meanwhile, without even a thank you, took the proffered report and turned once again to address the ex-Colonel in the next bed.

"Ah yes, about your operation, Mr Meldrum, pretty routine, but, barring complications, two months of really intensive care

133

afterwards, here on the ward of course, should allay all your fears. Your insurance seems to be all in order, so we'll discuss the financial side later. Not to worry!" As Evans then closed the conversation with his well practised little saccharin smile. The Sister returned to the two cups of tea. Seeing no blue pill and assuming that Doctor Evans had completed the task in her absence, she began to vigorously stir the liquid. All the time being very careful not to mix up the teaspoons. It was little points like that which made one a very good Ward Sister. The task at last completed to her satisfaction, she shook Joe into a bleary eyed wakefulness. As he opened his eyes, feigning surprise, she pressed into his faltering hands the cup which sat nearest to his bed.

As Joe began mechanically, to sip his hot tea, he suddenly became aware of the hovering Doctor Boyle's sad, sorrowful gaze. He smiled reassuringly back at Boyle, then watched, with furtive fascination, as the busy Sister handed Doctor Evans the remaining cup of tea. His own cup emptied at last, Joe carefully replaced it on top of his locker with a contented sigh. His eyes now drawn once more to the scene around the old Colonel's bed.

Doctor Evans finished his tea, laid the cup down beside Joe's and reached for his pen. He then lifted up his report sheet, checked his Rolex and was seemingly just about to anticipate the time and probable cause of Joe's retiral to the acherontic shades; when, dramatically, both pen and report slipped from his suddenly useless hands. Time, for Mr Evans seemed to have run its inevitable course.

The initial controlled panic having eventually subsided, they wheeled the prostrate Hospital Manager's inert body towards the Intensive Care Ward at a reckless rate of knots. With a flustered Doctor Boyle and the Ward Sister forming a familiar rear guard. Joe, as he surveyed the mounting chaos, sighed deeply.

It must have been all of half an hour later that Doctor Boyle returned, stopped beside Joe's bed, eyed the empty cups with unconcealed suspicion and then picked them up gingerly.

"Poor Doctor Evans, has he passed on then?" Joe's voice was a model of polite concern. Doctor Boyle's answer when it

134

eventually came, betrayed his emotional state.

"No not dead yet . . . still in Intensive Care . . . fighting, but he may not make it."

Joe wondering if Evans had pulled rank or gone private, shook his head in mock grief.

"Shame, poor man! But I suppose we must be realistic about these things. He was living in a tough old world and not really all that well equipped to fight it. All that fat must have made for some discomfort. Did you ever get the impression Doctor, that he was somehow or other losing the will to live?"

Doctor Boyle ignored the question and gazed down suspiciously at the recumbent Joe for a long searching moment. But the sad, almost beatific smile which creased the old man's lined face dispelled his lingering doubts. Poor old codger, if he only knew what had really happened to Evans. It had been one real major balls up! Doctor Boyle sighed audibly. Life sure turned out funny at times!

"Now about your operation Mr Gillan, there could be complications of course at your age. A 50/50 chance; what with those damned weeping piles. Have I your permission to proceed?"

"Of course Doctor, but only if I get permission to play the nags!" The planning gain conceded. Doctor Boyle carried the cups down the ward. His receding figure causing an orderly to start whistling, *Tea for Two*. As he caught sight of the closely held cups. Joe, in turn picked up his *Daily Record* Newspaper with renewed enthusiasm. So today was the 250th Anniversary of the Battle of Culloden. He'd have to see if there was a horse named 'Prince Charlie' starting at Newmarket . . . there wasn't! He eventually plumped instead for two horses called 'Passion For Life', and 'Get Away With It'. A double which somehow or other summed up for Joe his present day's activities. And if the going stayed good to firm, it would soon be the bloody bookies who were, metaphorically speaking, 'weeping piles'. A little joke of Joe's he wished somehow that old Alf had been around to enjoy.

19

A Dried Up Source

Turning off the jungle path which he had been following since sun-up, Pedro threw himself to the ground in the small clearing he had glimpsed through his sweat and dust caked eyes.

Satisfied with his progress, he sighed contentedly, relaxing his bronzed body in the tree-shaded warmth of the noon-day Chilean sun. Impulsively kicking off the old canvas shoes which encased his feet, he began to piece together in his mind the happenings of the previous six days.

It had all started when Maria's mother arrived at their shack, aggressively demanding the return of the 150 pesos which he had borrowed from her some time previously to help buy a llama. Its fetlocks had on inspection shown traces of foot rot however, probably caused by long periods of work in the Lake Poopo area, so he hadn't bought the llama after all.

The money had instead been the source of many enjoyable evenings at the cantina. Then the old crone had made her appearance, demanding the money back. What on earth had possessed him to marry into such a family?

On arriving home from the cantina those six evenings past, and being confronted with her punitive aggressiveness and raving demands, things had started to go wrong. He had thrown the raddled, clawing, black-clad bundle of bones which was Maria's mother towards a stool in the corner of the shack.

His aim however, impaired by excessive tequila intake, had left much to be desired, and she had finished up a still, huddled heap, her head having made violent contact with the plough, which was leaning against the rear wall. Even before Maria, who had been sitting in another corner of the shack with that well-known stubborn look on her face, had sprung protectively towards her mother with a despairing, "Oh, Madre mia," they had somehow sensed that she was dead.

Between them they had lifted the old woman's body on to the bed, with a gentleness which she had never been shown during her lifetime, then Maria, her eyes yellow with hatred, had thrown on her shawl and made for the door, muttering the word "policia" as she went.

He hadn't meant to hit her, not his Maria, but something had to be done, and quickly, to stop her from losing her head completely. They had struggled for about three minutes before his hands on her throat had felt her body go limp, and the only resistance left had been in her eyes. In another moment even that, too, had died.

"It was a good job I didn't panic," he mused aloud, the sun's rays as they penetrated the foliage leaving slowly moving patterns of light on his faded denim suit and sweat-damp singlet. The next step now was to get to Mindores.

Since hurriedly leaving the locked cabin with its gruesome contents he had been travelling along the Andean passes and jungle tracks for six days, having crossed the border from his native Bolivia three days past at an unmanned border point, each step through this neighbouring country, Chile, bringing him nearer to the sea and safety.

Clearings similar to his present one had been his resting-places each night; what fruit and nuts he could lay his hands on as he hurried along being his only sustenance. In a few hours he would be at the port; for hadn't he caught a brief glimpse of it from a ridge a few kilometres back?

There, he hoped to stow away on a ship bound for the States. His cousin Jose, who worked at the port, would help to find the right ship. Jose was a capitan; at least, that was what he had said he was when they had been drinking the last of his mother-in-law's loan in the pueblo cantina on the night of the tragedy.

Towards sunset Pedro finally broke through the protective

covering of the jungle onto the beach. Using the seawood and flotsam which marked the high sideline as a carpet, for he detested the irritating feel of sand in his shoes, he followed the coastline towards the port. He paused only once, to examine with a landsman's interest the vicious claws of a large crab carcase which had been washed ashore and lay just clear of the darkening blue waters as they gently lapped the sands.

There was one ship in the harbour; he could now see its masts dwarfing the sun-dried waterfront shacks and sheds which combined to make up the port of Mindores. No activity disturbed the stillness of the darkening quay.

He smiled as he saw the Stars and Stripes drooping limply from the stem jack-mast of the freighter-things were working out very well indeed. The vessel appeared to be deserted, no light showed at any of her ports, but wasn't this all to his advantage?

At the bottom of the gangway, propped against an oil drum, was a red-painted notice-board bearing a white skull and crossbones emblem and some words. Pedro couldn't read the faded words in the gathering darkness; he could move stealthily, however, and, crouching low, he made his way up the wooden gangway, his body blending with the shadows.

At the top he glanced swiftly fore and aft along the ship's length, then made for the forward hold, the nearest place of safety in his present precarious position. Between the winches, where a hatch board had been removed, he climbed over the coaming. His groping foot quickly found the iron ladder which lead to the depths of the hold, and safety.

He hadn't needed to contact cousin Jose after all. Just as well, he thought, for Jose always seemed to extract a tequila toll for any favours he bestowed on his friends.

"Things will work out better in the States," he decided, settling his weary body down on some bales of gunny bags which he had encountered in the protective darkness.

". . . Hadn't Maria's brother made a fortune in New York before coming home to open the cantina where he, Pedro, had spent his last evening in the pueblo? There was no reason why he couldn't make his fortune also. He could never come back

138

to this area, of course, being a wanted man, but there were other places . . ."

With this thought bringing its crumb of comfort to his tired mind he fell into a sound sleep. Neither the replacing of the hatch board nor the swish of the tarpaulin as the hold was sealed off disturbed his slumbers.

When the cyanide fumigation canisters dropped silently through the vents on to the bales of gunny bags it was then too late for anyone to try.

At seven o'clock next morning, it should have been six, Pedro's cousin Jose woke with a start, cursed his English alarm clock for its unreliability, and struggled his fat frame into his old khaki uniform.

Arriving at the American freighter he quickly removed the fumigation notice which he had placed at the foot of the gangway and hurried aboard the lifeless ship. Once there he donned his gasmask – left lying from the previous evening – and began to sweep up those rats which had reached the deck before being finally overcome by the deadly fumes.

Down in the holds their companions, caught by the swiftness of the fatal cloud, lay in all the unposed attitudes which are associated with sudden and horrible death.

Jose, as ports fumigating officer, was expected to clean out the holds also, but sleeping in had upset his timetable. The crew would be returning to the ship in a couple of hours; he would just have time to remove the tarpaulins and air the holds and accommodation before they arrived to make ready for sea.

His decision to leave the holds didn't worry Jose unduly, however; it wasn't the first time that those damned gringos had to sweep up their own rats.

His tasks finally completed, Jose removed the gas mask from his by now heavily perspiring face, and stood pondering for a moment on the gangway.

He had sixteen pesos in his pocket, enough to take him back to his pueblo for the week-end on the train. No ships were due in for fumigation for the next four days, so there was really nothing to stop him from making the journey.

"Cousin Pedro is always. good for a jug of tequila," he reflected. "He likes to think that he's drinking with a real live capitan." He laughed bitterly. "If only he knew that I'm capitan of the Mindores rats."

He spat disgustedly towards the dark well of the forward hold and, walking slowly down the gangway, threw his gas mask and brush into the little wooden hut, situated between two storage sheds, which served as his place of business. He closed and locked the door, then strolled casually, hands in pockets, along the quay towards the railway junction. There to await the noisy old train which clanked and groaned its way each day through Chile, and on up to his native Bolivian pueblo.

Already the climbing sun was beginning to make him feel thirsty.

20

The Symposium at Hodge's Cross

It's good to flip the pages of memory once in a while. Early in my book of life I sometimes run across balmy summer evenings which were the spring of existence. In those days we lads from the townlands of Cabra, Monagor, Derry Island and other places, which time alas has dimmed to forgetfulness, used to congregate at Hodge's Cross. The crossroads, with its gently sloping banks falling gracefully down to the roadside, was an ideal lounging place for that illustrious gathering of sagacious youth which we laid claim to represent.

The hens housed, the last cow milked, and the last pig hurriedly fed and styed, there would be a hasty mounting of bicycles and a general graduation towards the cross. The bikes, many of them held together by string and hope, would be strewn along the upper banking, and we would take possession of the lower area of the roadside itself. There, to kick off our evening's entertainment, we would convince ourselves, with the big talk of callow youth, that Monaghan was the greatest county God gave to Ireland. And that its inhabitants weren't far behind.

When we had exhausted that subject to our satisfaction – and sure, it was easy to do that, for weren't we all in agreement? – we would then pass learned judgement on the rest of life's problems with the enthusiastic ignorance of the young. At that age, you see, we knew everything.

One in our midst would be codded to blushing embarrassment

about his courting of Paddy McShane's wall eyed daughter. The one with the fine figure, which she evidently must have kept in the bank. Then, that subject eventually palling, we would all concentrate on another's fall from grace under the misguiding influence of Sean Barleycorn. That subject too being, figuratively speaking, sucked dry, there would be a concerted turning towards the road at our feet for further entertainment and enlightenment. And, Irish country roads being the very personal highways that they are, we wouldn't have very far to look.

The girls, as they headed home from the shoe factory, or into Castleblayney to meet the latest beau on their string, were our favourite target. As they rode past on their bicycles, the barrage of good-natured advice we doled out to them just had to be heard to be believed; as they were all known to us, our advice was naturally tailored to their individual requirements. Some of the plainer girls slowed down perceptibly as they reached the cross, ready to glory in their brief moment of limelight, I suppose. Others, like teacher McQuade's daughter, for instance, always pedalled quickly past with tight little smiles on their faces. I always wondered why their social standing put the harness on their sense of humour. The real bigwigs mustn't have been able to raise a laugh at all. But we country boys just couldn't hope to compete with that class of people at their own level, our descent would have been far too abrupt.

Local farmers were another butt for our friendly banter. Every evening, as they rattled home from town in their laden, lazy assed carts, a few were jeeringly challenged to come down and give their struggling ass a wee bit of assistance, a wag in our midst butting in with, "Yea, let's see you make an ass of yourself!" Meanwhile, others would be made acquaint, whether they wanted them or not, with our humble opinions of their latest livestock purchases. The pigs and fowl usually stared curiously out at us from the farm grimed, slat-walled carts, while bovine purchases ambled along in front, hurriedly snatching at roadside tufts as they passed. The farmers treated our brash opinions with the good-natured scorn which was their due.

An odd time we used the crossroads as a rendezvous for

fishing expeditions to Loch Eigish. But we got into hot water up there, and we didn't even have to get wet to manage it. There was an old Colonel lived on the lochside, and as the best pool was near his cottage, we used to cod him a lot whenever he came on the scene. He went to one of these continental health resorts every winter, and they tell me he looked a picture of health when he eventually died. Another antagonist of ours was old Peader Murtagh. He fished the loch for pike, Japanese fashion, using a kite to carry his line out to the centre. Once, when his back was turned, some member of our bicycle expedition severed his line and the kite nose-dived into deep water. We were the cause of a lot of grief up at the loch, I suppose. But it didn't last long, for the fishing, like all our other youthful 'ploutherings' about, was only a passing notion.

But it's time now to get on to the serious part of the story. All had gathered at the cross as usual one September evening and were basking in the fading heat of the dying sun – which in those days still shone in September. We had exhausted the personal subjects, the road was unusually quiet, and languorous boredom was threatening to take over. Then, out of the fading blue, Dinty Woods, a junior member of our group, piped in with an ear pricking suggestion.

"Let's run a best joke contest!"

Knowing Dinty, we should have caught on that he had something special up his tattered sleeve. But we took the bait, each of us confident that the joke we told was going to win the prize in any roadside talent contest.

There must have been eighteen of us there that evening. Dinty passed his cap round, and after a bit of lending and promising, we managed to put in an old penny each. The cap was then ceremoniously placed in our midst and, our throats dry with the excitement of it all, the contest got under way.

Talk about old jokes! Some of those told that evening made the Battle of the Boyne front page news in the *Monaghan Argus*. Mickey O'Hare kicked off with the one about an American tourist, appropriately named Theophilus Noyes, who told the old Irishman that he could board a train in Texas and still be in the

143

same state twelve hours later. To which his yawning listener replied that they had trains like that in Ireland too. It must have been funny first time round, I suppose, but in this talent studded contest it only earned a polite titter from the viewing contestants.

After about twelve of us had told our jokes, with varying degrees of success, Black Pat Duffy's son, Red Michael, was in a very challenging position. He was going north for his holidays. When one of them asked him if the climate might not disagree with his wife, his sarcastic rejoinder had been that it wouldn't dare try. This effort had, at that stage, raised the biggest laugh. There were a few more desperate attempts to land the prize money, the most notable of these being Joe Dolan's political one about the two Irishmen who were bemoaning the sad state of their native land. In a moment of inspiration, one had suggested that Ireland should declare war on America, and when they beat the ould country, they'd feel so sad about it that they'd pour in the dollars by the billions to help Ireland re-build. To which the other Irishman had replied pessimistically, "Fair enough, but what happens if we beat them?"

And then young Dinty, who had been silent to the very last, cleared his throat and came in with what we voted that night to be the greatest joke that ever came out of the county bar none. And to those who are still with me, I make no apologies for repeating his masterpiece, word for word.

"Me father," began Dinty, wearing his cod serious expression, "was one of the many sons of Erin who wandered over to England to broaden their minds and narrow their outlooks. On the night before he was due to go, it was decided to hold a ceilidh and, for the excuse, they said it was to celebrate his departure. Well, it got under way all right, but in the midst of the festivities that night, me father happened to stagger accidentally into a corner behind the jamb wall in Hannigan's kitchen. And there didn't he find Mrs Dunne from up the bog lane standin' there cryin' her eyes out. It was a real sad sight on an otherwise gay night. And, full of porter and goodwill, he went over to comfort the old lady.

" 'Houl' on there, Mrs Dunne. Sure, a little sliver like yourself shoudn't have to carry all that sorrow on your own. What say you lay some of it on my oul' back?'

"Within two minutes she was eagerly tellin' him the whole story.

"It seemed that Neilly, her only son, had gone to England nearly six months before, and she hadn't had the scrape of a pen from him from that day till then. She didn't even know if he was still alive. The cruel heartless shame of it.

"Well, to make a long story even longer," continued Dinty dramatically. "Me father promised her before all the saints in heaven, as well as the few in hell, that if she would only dry her eyes and enjoy the ceilidh, he would contact the wayward Neilly as soon as he reached England. And would he give that gasoon a piece of his mind!"

At this point Red Michael ventured that, knowing Dinty's father, the old fellow must have given Neilly at least half of it. Dinty cast a scathing glance at Red Michael, shook his head sadly, and then continued to tell his story.

"The only information me father could get from Mrs Dunne that night was that Neilly had gone to a place in London called WC2 it was a slim lead. But he reiterated his promise and then got the much happier Mrs Dunne up for *The Walls of Limerick* and *The Dashing White Sergeant*." Dinty paused for a recollective moment.

"Me father arrived in England stoned. (He's been stoned more times than the Russian Embassy since then, incidentally.) And, remembering his promise to Mrs Dunne, he travelled to London and got fixed up in lodgings; a place called Shaftesbury Avenue, I think it was. Once he was settled, he signed on for work, and then started his search. Well, for weeks he searched, but nobody in Rooney's Tavern could tell him where the district was. Nor was there hint or hair of Neilly.

"One wet evenin', filled with a happy sort of despair, he wandered into the toilet at Victoria Station for a little relief. About to leave a couple of minutes later, he happened to glance at the row of small rooms which lined the far wall of the toilet. There, right in front of his honest Irish eyes, was one marked WC2. He blinked in disbelief, then looked again. It was still there, he had

145

g

at last caught up with the elusive Neilly. Talk about the luck of the Irish! The pent up frustration of weeks of fruitless searching welled up in me father's breast, as he marched, with just the tiniest hint of alcoholic swagger mark you, up to that door marked WC2. His clenched fist rat-tat-tatted on the panel as he shouted impatiently.

"Are you Neilly Dunne in there?"

"I am," an anxious voice answered from within, "but I've no paper."

"Well now, isn't that the poor excuse for not writing to your poor, cryin' oul' mother back home in Ireland."

For all of five minutes we laughed our heads off at Dinty's joke. We then gave him the money, for what else could you do to a young bucko who gives out with quality yarns like that? Dinty, we all agreed then, would go far. But not in the same way as his father – all the old bucko was famous for was a hard neck. He admitted having it, but contended that he got it with carrying the hod on nearly every building site in England. I dare say you'll have run into him at some time or other over there?

Ah! Weren't those the days, my friend? Like Dinty's oul' man I travelled across the water to seek fame and fortune. It took me ten years to save me fare back to the land of Conn again – but who could go home without making a pilgrimage to Hodge's Cross? Alas for sentimental journeys – they'd turned the whole area into a monster of a pigmeal factory. What a memorial to those happy days. I ask you, pigmeal!

I was standing in the loading bay of the factory, feeling a right sucker as you might say, just wondering where the cross had disappeared to. I heard a noise behind me and, as I turned round, this fellow comes rushing out of the factory. He's all spruced up with a collar and tie, and starts to shake me by the hand. It takes me half a minute to realise it's the same Dinty – he's the factory manager now, and a father of three. I noticed that he wasn't smiling nearly half as much as he used to. But that's progress, I guess. We stood there raking up old times till the factory closed for the night. As the youngsters came out on their bicycles, I heard one shout to his companion, "I'll meet you up at Conlon's

Cross about seven."

So it looks as if they've moved the cross a wee bit and changed the name when they were at it. But as long as Ireland has meeting places like these, and lads of the calibre of Dinty to grace them, all is not yet lost in that fair land.

21

The Whole Thing's Monstrous

We had called Alec's previous car his polite car — for it had raised its battered bonnet to nearly every garage mechanic in Scotland. While I checked off the camping list, I was silently praying that his latest acquisition was in a more dependable condition.

"And last, but not by any means least, the camera tripod. We'd better not forget that."

Alec closed the boot of the old Rover and I pocketed the camping list. The dreaded moment had arrived. "Right, let's get moving, Joe. We've only a weekend to establish beyond doubt the existence of that confounded monster up in Loch Ness."

I followed him into the car, we settled ourselves, the engine roared into life and away we went on a monster hunt. As Glasgow's neon lit horizon faded behind us, I shook my head in disbelief. Friday nights I usually reserved for a dance session, or maybe a visit to the cinema. But Alec was a real persuasive guy. Now, as he drove determinedly out through Hardgate, I gathered together my scattered thoughts and peered reluctantly at the tattered route map.

By the time we reached Balloch it was really getting dark. Undaunted, we twisted our way up the Loch Lomond road to Crianlarich. It started to rain as we passed through that sleepy little town. But we moved northwards through the downpour, doggedly determined to reach our destination. The moon had retired, defeated. And all we could do now was chase the twin beams of the headlamps as they carved a tunnel of light into the night blackness. Round about midnight, Alec, with a stifled yawn, asked casually, "How about stopping somewhere and knocking up a meal on the stove, Joe?"

"Oh, let's get there first, Alec," I countered hastily. "Only another couple of hours and we'll be in the land of Nessie."

"OK, suit yourself. But you've just turned down the meal of a lifetime. My moments of culinary greatness don't hang around, you know."

I gave a shudder of relief. Alec's an inspired blender of canned victuals. His efforts, sampled on previous trips, had been enough to make Fanny Craddock turn in her gravy.

Some time later, the road now a waterlogged ribbon seeming to twist and turn towards oblivion, we began to feel tired. But we pressed on, me poring over the map by torch-light and passing on directions. Around about two in the morning we reached the water's edge, exceptionally good going despite the prevailing conditions.

The rain now being, if anything, worse, we hastily decided to abandon the cooking idea and grab a few hours shut-eye in the car instead. As I made myself comfortable in the rear, Alec, already stretched out in front, switched on the radio. All at once the peaceful patter of the rain on the roof was swamped by a raucous rhumba from a canned band. I groaned inwardly. But there was more to come. The announcer stopped the music, and began to tell a joke about cannibals. But to me it was in poor taste, and I'm no vegetarian. I closed my eyes and being very tired, slept.

I shivered into wakefulness in the dawn light. As I tenderly unravelled the crick in my neck, I discovered that Alec had already pitched the tent and, by the light of the rising sun, was circling the roaring Calor stove. A can-opener gleamed malevolently in his grubby hand. Apprehensive, I staggered out, made for the car boot and unearthed a bottle of whisky. I've always believed that one swallow doesn't make an alcoholic. So I was just elevating the bottle for the second gulp when Alec shouted over.

"Come on, Joe, lay off that stuff. You know we've a hard day ahead of us with the telescopes and the cine-camera."

I suddenly remembered what we had come up to this area for. Awed, I turned and gazed out over the forbidding strip of dancing waters under whose depths lurked the great orm. A legendary creature offered to a sceptical world by suspect camera work, inspired hearsay and gospel rumour. But this weekend would see an end to all the doubts. For weren't Alec and I on the job? In a gesture of self-congratulation I absentmindedly raised the bottle to my lips once more.

"Watch it, Joe!"

I hurriedly lowered the bottle. Alec's one of those straight-laced types. There are four churches in the street where he resides – talk about living in a chastity belt! Much to the cook's annoyance I feigned sickness and dodged breakfast. Well, would you fancy a breakfast of tinned curry and tripe?

After breakfast there was a great deal of running up hill and down glen before we eventually got the camera sited in a corrie overlooking a long stretch of the loch. We then hefted the hired telescopes to adjoining heights and began to eagerly range the sunlit waters. But nothing stirred.

Along about three in the afternoon my eyes were all strained to hell and the drained, rejected whisky bottle lay dead at my feet. But it had braced me against another attack of Alec's cooking. I scrambled a wee bit unsteadily back to the car. He watched me proudly as I forced down a helping of his latest culinary effort, sardines and ravioli. Ugh! He elevated a questioning eyebrow. With bulging mouth I raised a reluctant thumb. A much milder gesture than a verbal lie.

The punishment eventually ended however. And we were just contemplating a belated return to the telescopes when, with a rustle of wet undergrowth, the whins beside the tent parted. An ancient highland laddie, wearing a makeshift cloak of tattie-bag tweed over his head and shoulders, now intruded his dram fresh countenance into our midst. A shepherd, no doubt, recognisable by his four-legged badge of office, a collie dog.

"Guid day, men! And wid there be a wee bittie left in the pot?"

The only time a Scotsman is really at home is in someone else's. As Alec rushed to oblige, horrified, I shut my eyes. But that shepherd guy was no mean diplomat. After he had sampled the first spoonful of Alec's speciality his face crimsoned. The plate of leftovers dropped from his seemingly clumsy hands and the dog tore in.

"Oh, ah'm sorry. Verra clumsy of me. But ma dog'll see it's no wasted. Hamish'll eat anything," he ended apologetically, by way of explanation of the dog's behaviour. "Ah suppose you lads'll be up in the highlands for the fishin'?"

"Well, not really," I answered. Then I raced on, a challenging note now creeping into my voice. "We've come North to get some pictures of the monster."

"Oh, ye've heard aboot that beastie then?"

"Of course, who hasn't? The Loch Ness monster's now world property. Better known even than Rabbie Burns."

"Och ay, richt enough. The Loch Ness beastie's very famous," his voice held a strange note of relief. "Well, all the best, laddies. I'll hae to go now, for by the sound of them ma sheep are gettin' a wee bittie restless."

As unexpectedly as he'd come, he disappeared back into the heathery undergrowth, his dog at his wellingtoned heels.

Alec and I, now behind schedule, rushed to take up our belated stations at the telescopes.

At first I put it down to the drink! I rubbed my eyes and then tried to put the blame on my mate's cooking. But still the incredible vision persisted. At first, it had looked for all the world like the inquisitive periscope of a submarine. But its small head, balanced on a long powerful neck, now stretched all of fifteen feet out of the leaden grey water. At this stage it was clearly visible even to the naked eye. Oh, if only I could reach the camera before it submerged again! I hastily abandoned the telescope and raced for the crag where we'd sited the camera. But Alec, bless him, had beaten me to it. On arrival, breathless and excited, I discovered that he already had the cine-camera rolling and was feverishly zooming into close-up position.

The body of the monster, looking to all appearances like that of a huge elephant, was now clearly visible; in all it must have been at least thirty feet long, ending in a short, tapering tail. The

151

camera motor whirred busily as Alec followed every unhurried movement of that great orm, last surviving link with some strange, bygone era. Then tragedy struck – the film roll came to an end. I grabbed a roll of stills and fed them through while Alec carefully stowed the cine reel away. Soon the still film, too, was exhausted. There wouldn't be time to return to the car for fresh supplies. As if sensing our frustration, the great monster casually swivelled its head in our direction, made a noise somewhere between a dog bark and a cow cough, and then slowly disappeared into the depths of the loch. As far as it was concerned, the show was over.

But we now had on film the most explosive scene ever to hit the world headlines. Alec, ever impetuous, was all for racing back to civilisation and selling out to the highest bidder. I counselled caution, however. After all, if we played our cards right at this stage, we could retire for life.

Elated, I even enjoyed Alec's cooking that night. Except for the ants, that is. If they're so industrious, how come they manage to take in all the picnics? After supper, despite his glance of disapproval, I had a wee tot from my standby bottle. Then we turned in early, for tomorrow we had a long scoot south ahead of us. I fell asleep dreaming of the distillery which I was going to open with the proceeds from my world lecture tour. In honour of our monster I would label the product 'Great Ness' – a clever touch that. And the fiery spirit would become better known in America than even blueberry pie or that Watergate guy. Such is the stuff of dreams. That night I slept the sleep of the righteous. When I awoke, the sun was slicing through a torn cloud. A wonderful omen?

We had breakfasted – ugh! – stowed everything away, and were just getting ready to move off, when our highland friend did a reappearing act from the lochside shrubbery.

"Well, hello there!" I greeted him good-humouredly. "I hope you found your sheep all right yesterday?"

"Och, ay, man, they were fine – chust fine. Ah suppose this'll be you two off tae Loch Ness tee speir for the monster? Chust turn right when you reach the fork, ye canna miss it, it's only aboot twenty miles up the glen."

Alec and I were by this time exchanging puzzled glances. I had been navigator. The pit of my stomach began to play tricks.

"Isn't this Loch Ness then?" I asked guardedly, as I pointed to the brooding water lapping almost at our feet.

"No' really, mannie. That's Loch Laggan. We've a wee beastie in there, too. But we dinna like tee advertise the fact too much, so dinna let oan ah telt ye. Fur too many veesitors wid maybe upset the sheep. Especially at lambin' time."

He watched, puzzled, as weak-knee'd, we moved towards the old Rover, all the time exchanging broken, defeated glances. If the world was still sceptical about the Loch Ness monster after all these years, what chance had the Loch Laggan monster of making the headlines? Not a duck's chance on treacle!

But we'd have to try. Alec gunned the motor and we moved bumpily off, followed by the excited barking of the collie and an encouraging, "Hope ye find Nessie!" from that darned old Sheikh of Sheepville.

When we eventually reached Glasgow, the wires hummed. In adjoining telephone booths we phoned around desperately trying to hawk our exclusive story, with pictures, of the Great Orm of Loch Laggan. We badgered nearly every newspaper in the business. But no joy! The incredulous answers ranged from, "You should give up the Sunday drinking, old boy!" to "You're nothing but a pseudo intellectual bigot trying to inject into susceptible society your own particular brand of cultured venom." Phew! That lady from the Bognor Regis *Bugle* sure sounded peeved.

When, at last, we stumbled, defeated, from Queen Street Station's now red hot telephone kiosks, night had come. Alec, looking sick, said he was going to make for home – I let him. When he'd driven off, I wandered into a hotel to forget that disastrous trip. When I eventually left it, the moon was high and so was I. My sorrow drowned, where now? The cab driver suggested I put in some dancing at the Rec. Hall. With a slurred "Lead off, McDuff," I settled back.

The Rec. Hall should have been renamed the 'Wreck Hall'. From the door of that smoke box filled with multi-coloured jumping beans I surveyed the noisy scene. Then I caught a glimpse of this dark-eyed frail with a ponytail. I don't believe in horsing around, and a few moments later we had joined the rest of the frenzied floor frolickers. I threw out my opening gambit.

"Come here often?"

"Naw, the place is deid!"

She spoke like she was capable of being illiterate in at least seven different languages. At this juncture I also noticed that she was one of those girls who are incapable of standing on their own two feet. Did she apologise? Not on your life. Her next communication nearly floored me.

"Can ye no' dance, Mack?"

Well, I ask you! And me a gold medallist from the Dan McWhirter school of dancing too. But I ignored the verbal attack, parrying with a placatory, "Where are you holidaying this year?"

"Italy at the Fair. A gigolo pinched me in the Pantheon last year. Oh, it was rare," her face had lit up with the memory of it all.

I suppose that in a predicament like that you merely turned the other cheek?"

"Och, ay."

My little gem of repartee having passed, unnoticed, I sadly danced on in a bored, mechanical fashion, impatiently waiting for the dance to end. I was sobering up. And memories of Loch Laggan were creeping back.

Out in the fresh night air at last, I began to stumble towards home. Here were Alec and I sitting on a gold mine and no takers. If only I, as navigator, hadn't taken a wrong turning in the dark! If that old shepherd hadn't butted his nose in, we wouldn't have known the difference. A case of ignorance being bliss. I silently offered the old man a choice stream of invective. But it improved matters very little.

We're not beaten yet, however. Some day someone somewhere will officially recognise the existence of the Loch Laggan monster. Till then, however, if you'd like an illustrated lecture on that big beastie, I'm your man. There'll be a small expense, of course – to help maintain our liquid assets as it were. I'm sure you'll understand.

23

One Can't Discount
the Rumours

Alf Boyce was friendly, fit and forty. Nearly everything about him was nice, his wife, his red sandstone detached out in the suburbs, and his managerial position in the local bank. There was one little, black cloud on his otherwise sunny horizon, however. It came in the form of his old Aunt Sarah; her health had literally packed in, leaving his dear wife Gladys to cope with her petulant frailty all day and every day. What worried him most was the fact that this problem might well hang around for many years to come, for the old dear, although now seventy-six, was showing no real signs of cashing in the proverbial cheques. If ever there was a good case for the extermination pill, old Sarah, with her whining, "Get me this, get me that, do this, don't do that!" was it. Yes, indeed, it was a real nagging situation. Because of it his social life was at the non-existent level, and that just wasn't going to do at all, at all.

As he walked briskly to the bank that Friday morning, Alf's computer-like mind was sorting and examining every aspect of his problem. Things were becoming really difficult, for the old witch had at three o'clock that very morning wakened them from a sound sleep and demanded, of all things, ice cream! To have her housed in a State institution might reflect very badly on his public image, so that solution was definitely not on. No! They must devise a way of getting her off their hands once and for all. Failing that, the best years of their lives would be spent playing nursemaid to the old crow.

The problem still kicking around in his mind, he was skirting Ellesmere marsh when he noticed that a small builder's hut with Council markings, had just been erected by the roadside. What was this then? An old watchman, already settled in, was brewing tea on a Calor stove. The acre of boggy pools, some nearly eight feet deep, was surely a strange venue for a builder's hut. Alf, as he came abreast of the old watchman, exclaimed cheerfully, "Morning, my good man! Surely the Council aren't really thinking of developing this area?" He waved his arm casually in the direction of the deep, reed-covered pools lying behind the hut.

"Good morning, sir! They are, indeed. Far as I know they're starting to fill in the marsh come Monday. Plannin' to build forty houses on the site, they are."

"About time too! For this area's a rate-payer's eyesore, a real disgrace to the village."

As the old watchman nodded agreement, Alf tipped his bowler, waved his folded brolly in farewell, and continued on his way to the bank.

It was nearly three hours later that the solution to his problem dawned on him. If they were going to start filling in the marsh area on Monday, anything deposited in one of the pools before that time was sure to be irretrievably buried under the rubble. Like old Aunt Sarah, for instance?

When, after dinner that evening, he guardedly broached the subject to Gladys, his wife, she exclaimed in a long-suffering voice, "No, Alf, not that! And anyway, it's too risky. I suppose I'll just have to go on putting up with the silly old witch."

But Alf persisted, and as he outlined his plan in his most persuasive voice, she gradually came round to his way of thinking. So much so that, when she took the old lady's nightcap up to her that evening, there was a triple dose of sleeping tablets in the warm beverage. When, two hours later, Alf went up to Aunt Sarah's room, holding the pillow over her face was a mere formality. It had been so simple after all — no fuss, no pain, a neat, tidy job. But the really difficult part was still ahead of them.

He went down to the garage, reversed out the car, then went

upstairs for the old lady's blanket-wrapped remains. How light she was! Gladys, who had always been complaining about the old dear's weight, mustn't be very strong, he decided. Alf gently carried her down to the car, laid the body on the rear seat, and then returned to the house. His wife had the rope ready and was in the process of bringing the weights, in the form of two discarded old fire-grates, up from the cellar. That would be ample, for it wouldn't take much to sink the frail old body of Aunt Sarah. Everything loaded, he then drove out through the darkness, stopping at the edge of the marsh farthest from the watchman's hut. A quick tiptoe check showed that the old fellow was fast asleep; a book, on the cover of which a lady was revealing everything but her age, lay by his side. Alf parted his lips and shook his head in silent disapproval. "At his age, too!" But the situation was all to the good. He quickly returned to the car, lifted the old lady out and carried her to the edge of the deepest pool he could find. A quick return trip for the weights, and a few deft hitches later she was sinking like a stone into the murky depths. Alf gazed into the dark pool for a moment with quiet satisfaction. Then, deciding he'd better not hang around, he returned to his car and drove home to the comforting arms of Gladys, his nice little wife.

For once they had a beautifully balanced weekend. With no Aunt Sarah worries, they went to the village dance on the Saturday evening – Alf really took a trick with his deft tango footwork. And on the Sunday evening, they had the Hetherington-Jones' over for dinner. If what they said about Mrs Hetherington-Jones was to be believed, Gladys's Waterford chandelier would soon be the talk of the village. During the weekend, Alf had subtly let it slip here and there that old Aunt Sarah had taken a sudden notion to finish her days with a niece over in Chipping Onger.

As he walked to work on the Monday morning, the murder already two days and two social functions old, Alf was feeling quite chirpy. Their cover story was good, all he'd have to do was cancel the old lady's pension at the post office, and that would be the proverbial that. For no one was going to check if she didn't reapply for it elsewhere. Yes, all in all, the set up looked pretty good. As he passed the watchman's hut, he was whistling quietly under his breath. A glance showed him that the oldster was in the middle of another of his innumerable cups of tea.

"Well, my good man, busy as usual, I see. I suppose these lorries will be turning up any minute now to start filling in the marsh? I only hope they don't mess up the road in the process!"

"Oh it's yourself, sir. A fine morning, if I may say so. I don't think there are going to be any lorries today after all. So you needn't fret about the state of the roads. The darned Council have gone and changed their ruddy minds again."

"What do you mean – gone and changed their minds again?" Alf was now having difficulty in controlling the lump in his throat.

"Well, it seems, sir, that their latest plan is to get the Fire Brigade to pump out the marsh to allow the surveyor to examine the bottom. If it's all right, they'll drive in piles and build two multi-storey blocks. These planners just can't make their minds up for two minutes, sir. God only knows what they'll think of next. Are you sure you're feeling all right, sir?"

But Alf had heard enough. Not trusting himself to answer, he waved a feeble farewell to the watchman and continued on his way to the bank. The old man, as he watched him depart, muttered, "Ignorant sod, can't answer a civil question," and then returned to his tea.

For Alf, this was Crunchville with a vengeance. His mind still working with cool, mathematical precision, he came to the unhappy conclusion that he was well and truly trapped. Damn those bunglers on the Council. When the pumps emptied the marsh, the old dear's body would be uncovered, and his casual hints about Aunt Sarah's departure for Chipping Onger would mean instant incrimination. He could visualise it all only too clearly.

The only thing he could really do now was to confess to the crime, saying he had coerced Gladys into helping him, and hope for a reduced jail sentence.

His mind made up, he wrote a hasty letter of resignation to the bank directors, tidied up, and posted the letter at lunch-time. Then, with bowed head, he faltered his way to the police station. No need to phone Gladys, she'd know soon enough.

As the police car arrived at the marsh, the first lorry load of rubble was being tipped into its murky depths. Alf, in his distraught state, took a long moment to appreciate the significance of the scene. The old watchman, however, as he hurried across to greet the policemen, was telling the whole world what he personally thought of it.

"Ruddy Council at it again. First they'll fill it in, then they'll drain it. Too expensive, so they'll go back to filling it in again. It'd take Solomon's lawyer to keep up with that ruddy lot!"

As he saw Alf step out of the car between two policemen, he smiled cheerfully. "Good morning again, sir. I didn't know you were attached to the police?"

Alf, feeling the handcuff biting into his left wrist, smiled cynically.

He didn't reply, however. For right at that moment in time he was trying to remember the name of the councillor in the village who took to do with Social Welfare. Wiggins! That was it. Fred Wiggins! He would have to contact him and try to get Gladys fixed up with a job while he was doing his stretch. The Home Help Department would be just up her street.

24

The Lazarus Enigma

Talk about the poverty trap! No, on second thoughts, better not, it hurt too much. Only the *Guardian* newspaper could manage objectivity with regard to that sort of situation. On reflection though, decided Taffy, things were not really all that terminal. He had his Social Security and enough rent assistance to keep Mrs Jones, his landlady, in a more or less constant state of affability.

But there must be more to life than standing still. Bored for some time now with his mundane existence, he had started to spend more and ever more time in the local library; searching frantically through its dog-eared tomes for the true meaning of life. He had, of course, toyed with religion, but it had all come down to the question of, which religion? And where, beyond his ken, lurked that mysterious, nebulous thing called faith? Humanism had proved to be equally unfathomable. Who needed a stance that refused to accept that most western morality had a religious source, and as for their libertarian ideals, yuk! He'd even trawled the history shelves in his search for enlightenment, but that too had ended in disappointment. Historians had either tended to suffer from 'written by the winner' syndrome, or alternatively, had adopted a 'follow my leader' stance in their right, left or centre analytical endeavours.

It was on the esoteric shelves that Taffy at last found something to stir the longings in his Celtic being. That was it! Transcendental, or, out of the body, experiences; OK, so they paid some lip-service to the Christian concept of soul. But they went even further than that. They opined that, with meditation and constant practice, one could in this present life desert the flagging body and mentally soar beyond the realm of mundane existence. Imagine it, real out of body experiences, all beyond the sordid, clapped out environment which was his present lot. It would require more than a modicum of meditation and practice of course, but he was doing nothing else anyway, and the results might be just what he was missing in his psyche. After all, the Dalai Lama rated it.

Following very carefully the various instructions, enlightenment gradually followed. The first time he managed to leave his body, this after a whole month of endeavour, he emitted a silent scream of joy. Total eureka; but gazing down on his still form there on the bed, the joyous moment was immediately followed by one of abject panic. What if there was no way back? But there was; meditating hard, he soon found himself back in, and a veritable prisoner of, his gradually re-awakening corpse.

By dint of concerted experimentation, he was soon managing to improve the technique. No longer just hovering about two feet above his body, he found that he could now rise to ceiling level. Even move cautiously to the far corner of the room. And on the day that he could actually leave the room that imprisoned his inert body, and eventually return with confidence, his joy became almost unbearable.

So began his spirit voyages, free entry to the local cinema, to a play in the big smoke, even to a pop concert by a gay icon up in Harrogate. But the latter experience didn't do much for him, and it was with a sense of relief that he returned to inhabit his forsaken body.

Taffy should have known that dates were going to be important in his new existence. If he had, he would not have decided to embark on a world tour on the last day of the month. January it was, and on impulse he set off, in spirit that was, to take in the follies in gay Paris. The enjoyment was so great that a detour to Amsterdam was almost eclipsed by his funkier experiences in Rome. He thought for a moment about returning home to his digs, but, man was he on a high! The following day found him gazing down upon the sidewalks of New York, before making a swift detour to Mexico City, Sydney and Tokyo. It was after sampling the delights of Peking that, temporarily sated, he turned once more towards home.

But meanwhile, in his absence, his trigger-happy landlady, Mrs Jones, noting his failure to promptly deliver the agreed room rental on time, decided, tight lipped, to instigate what one might describe as a financial confrontation. Having reassured herself that the inert body of Taffy was indeed moribund, the Law was summoned to sort out the obviously delicate state of affairs. Indeed, he was unfortunate in many ways. The previous tenant of Taffy's room had taken advantage of Mrs Jones's good nature and absconded owing three weeks rent. So when Taffy seemed to be displaying similar signs of financial constipation she had quite properly, but sadly for him, over reacted.

Taffy re-entered his room just as the black-suited undertakers were screwing the last brass nail into a plain, almost pauperish, pine coffin. He paused mentally to take stock. Christ! Was he seeing things, or was he seeing things? His immediate reaction had been to make a beeline for his inert self, which he could now observe despite the intervening pine coffin, but his mind counselled caution. There must be no hasty act at this delicate moment in time. If he had been any old libertarian humanist he could have waved a mental good riddance to his enclosed corpus, taken off with relief, and gone on metaphysically partying around the globe from here to eternity. But the harsh reality was that ethereal travelling, however enjoyable, tended to lose its kicks if one had no physical base to return to. There surely had to be some other way?

Meanwhile, as he gazed at the coffin's progress onto the waiting hearse, he noted cynically that his final departure was going to become one of those cheapo affairs he had often read about in the tabloids. No mourners, no flowers, not even Mrs Jones; right now he could envisage her composing the shop window advert that would attract her new tenant, and, to his mounting disgust, there wasn't even the proverbial brass nameplate on the economy model wooden box. As the French

162

might have said, "C'est la vie!" The unaccompanied hearse was now proceeding towards the cemetery with unseemly haste, there to finally come to a brake squealing halt before what was obviously a pauper's grave. At least he wouldn't feel alone in such communal surroundings.

But he couldn't just hang around here and do shit all to influence the rapidly deteriorating situation. From his extensive historical readings, he was now well aware of pitfalls associated with graveyard resting places. The American grave diggers for instance, who in '86, while charged with removing and re-interring coffins, had discovered with growing horror that at least ten per cent of the bodies had displayed various signs of frantic after burial activity. Was this alas to be his fate also? But there again, a perennial meander round the fleshpots of the world, albeit without his body was an equally disquieting scenario. It was now becoming patently obvious to him that out of body hedonism wasn't part of his makeup, that was for sure!

The grave digger, rudely short-cutting the funeral director's brief, mumbled eulogy, was already shovelling the clay earth over the coffin. To be, or not to be? Taffy's moment of decision had arrived. Filled with dread, but without hesitation, he quickly slid below the cloying earth, down, down to where, maybe, just maybe, his welcoming body would be awaiting the grand reunion.

25

The Human Element

After swiftly calculating a ten point fix on his new billion dollar Dekalog computer guiding system, Frank 'Georgia' Jackson corrected the course of his Astra five spacecraft by one micro minute and switched on the intercom.

"Hello, Earth, hello, Cape Wallace? Astra five space shot reporting. Over."

The Cape Wallace space centre answered almost immediately, its transmission set so clear that he had no difficulty in recognising the calm voice of Andy Wilson, the course plot chief.

"Come in, Astra five, receiving you loud and clear. Over."

"Hi, Andy! I'm now only five million miles from Mars. I'll undertake three orbits as planned before I land. Have you any further information for me? Over."

"We sure have Georgia Boy! The computer boys have been re-analysing the Astra Four tapes, and guess what! It's now positive that human life exists on Mars. How's that for good news? Over."

"Gee! Just great! I can't wait to get the Atmobug launched and go take a look see. Can you imagine it, man! I'll be the first guy to contact extra terrestrial humanity. Won't Mom be pleased? Over."

"She sure will, Georgia boy. But fade out now. We don't want to exhaust your solar batteries. Over and out."

'Georgia' Jackson pressed off the intercom button and relaxed once more into his shock couch. He was feeling just great after that brief contact with Andy Wilson. Here he was, poised less than five million miles from the most tremendous moment to date in history. Sure, the guys who'd made the moon had been lauded, and then some. But that dump had been dead, lifeless. This was the really big thing, actual contact with human life on another planet. Boy, would the name of Frank 'Georgia' Jackson go down in history! He settled back into his shock couch and began to daydream the journey away.

The Dekalog's warning bleep brought him quickly back to reality. Its pulsating red light indicated positive Martian gravity pull. He retroed the Astra craft onto an orbital course and began to thoroughly check the Atmobug. 'Georgia' worked carefully, for the bug, which the scientists had designed to optimum perfection, was going to be the vital link between the space craft and Martian civilisation. It contained just enough fuel for a brief period on the planet's surface and quick return to the Astra craft. Too light to carry earth link radio equipment, it would be the only hour or so in the whole expedition during which space centre communication with 'Georgia' would cease. Satisfied at last, he left the Atmobug and went on to check the colour television camera which would beam the first report to earth on his return from the planet to his spacecraft. He flashed himself a boyish smile on the monitor screen and then switched it off.

All set, the Dekalog indicated one more orbit to go and then the big moment. Wouldn't those Martians be surprised! They themselves hadn't yet managed a contact flight to earth, so the way 'Georgia' figured it was that he was a sort of emissary of progress to an unenlightened galaxy of the universe. 'Emissary of progress' – not a bad phrase that, a good title for his biography when he came to cashing in on his fame. He checked the chronometer. Ten minutes to dropout. He'd better make a final check with the space centre in case there were any last minute instructions. Andy Wilson's voice came in right away.

"Glad to hear from you again, Georgia boy. Remember to switch on the television camera as soon as you return from the planet to Astra craft. And we'll home in on you as planned from this end. You'll have a real big audience, so we'll be expecting that famous smile of yours. Good luck now – over and out."

So that was that. From now on he was on his own. He squeezed past the Dekalog, climbed into the Atmobug, and began to prepare for the secondary count down. He had practised this stage so often before at the space centre that the next hour or so held no terrors for him. It would be all routine. 'Georgia' leaned over and casually pressed the launch button, his marble white finger as steady as a rock.

Back on earth, by means of a cleverly strung series of orbiting telstars, American communications experts were reckoning that a colossal audience of nearly two thousand million people around the globe would be watching that first dramatic transmission from the Astra craft. A much needed prestige boost for Uncle Sam. Everything now prepared, the space centre staff had just time to grab a quick meal before homing in on the triumphant 'Georgia' boy.

Not all the viewers had hopeful expectation stamped on their faces however. For, as with people, whenever a nation dares to walk tall, there are neighbours of a sort who would gladly see it fall. At last the big moment came. From the Indian ocean area to the Pacific seaboard, people rose early or stayed up late, dependent on what time of day it was in their particular burg, to witness the historical event.

The programme opened appropriately with the rousing strains of *Marching Through Georgia*. The camera meanwhile was taking the viewers on a guided tour of 'Georgia' Jackson's home, and throwing in shots of the known universe for good measure – real solid build up material. Then the President, much more refined now than in his fiery governorship days, threw in his five cents worth about America's young galaxial emissary of peace and progress. The preliminaries now over, Andy Wilson cut in the tiny knife switch which would beam the world into the Astra craft piloted by proud Martianaut Frank 'Georgia' Jackson.

Reception was instantaneous and brilliantly clear; right on cue, 'Georgia' was safely back in his Astra craft shock couch. But something had gone seriously wrong. For where was that earth captivating 'Georgia' boy smile? Andy Wilson, in a desperate attempt to remove the sour, disappointed look from Frank

Jackson's face, opened up a hasty programme saving commentary, his voice oozing forced happiness, a saccharin smile on his worried face.

"Well, here he is, folks – the boy from Georgia, USA, who has this day made extra terrestrial history. What this young emissary of progress and human democracy has accomplished today will go a long way towards shaping the world of tomorrow. Now, Georgia boy – could you please tell us in your own words just what you saw on the planet Mars today?

At this point the whole scene became too much for Frank Jackson. He buried his head in his hands, and the camera focus was so perfect, that the tears of chagrin which escaped through his marble white fingers, could even be followed as they dripped slowly down the glass face of his new billion dollar Dekalog. For a brief moment it seemed to the viewers as though it, too, had been in some way upset by the whole strange proceedings. Then, lowering his trembling hands, his taut mouth now a hard red line on his very shocked white face, Frank 'Georgia' Jackson, stumbled at last onto his cue. He blurted out savagely, in front of his expectant audience of some two hundred million assorted Earthlings: "What did I see? I saw niggers down there, Andy. Nothing but millions of Goddam happy, smiling coons. The lousy planet's crawlin' with the no good bums. Gimme a course plot, fella. I'm gettin' to hell outa here. But fast!"